ABOUT THIS BOOK

Welcome to Havenwood Falls, a small town in the majestic mountains of Colorado. A town where legacies began centuries ago, bloodlines run deep, and dark secrets abound. A town where nobody is what you think, where truths pose as lies, and where myths blend with reality. A place where everyone has a story. Including the high schoolers. This is only but one . . .

Ivy Rapha has always been a dutiful daughter, never questioning the faith-healing con her parents have been pulling for as long as she can remember. At 17, she's stood by her whole life, watching them swindle innocent people out of small fortunes. But when she inexplicably gains actual healing powers, she runs away before her parents can exploit her. Her path leads her to a mysterious town in the mountains, where she hopes to find redemption for her part in the façade and learn to use her new gift in earnest.

Justus Abbadon is a demon with a big problem: he has a conscience. As a new Havenwood Falls High graduate, he's desperate to find a way out of his obligation to go into the family business. When Ivy arrives in Havenwood Falls and quickly finds herself at the snarling end of a wolf shifter, Justus steps in and seizes the opportunity to prove he's more than his conniving father's son.

As they both search for a way to redeem their past and find their purpose, they'll discover that the journey to redemption is marked by great sacrifice. No one arrives unscathed, and reclaiming their souls may end up costing their lives.

RECLAMATION

A HAVENWOOD FALLS HIGH NOVELLA

ANNALISA GRANT

HAVENWOOD FALLS HIGH BOOKS

Written in the Stars by Kallie Ross
Reawakened by Morgan Wylie
The Fall by Kristen Yard
Somewhere Within by Amy Hale
Awaken the Soul by Michele G. Miller
Bound by Shadows by Cameo Renae
Inamorata by Randi Cooley Wilson
Fata Morgana by E.J. Fechenda
Forever Emeline by Katie M. John
Reclamation by AnnaLisa Grant
Avenoir by Daniele Lanzarotta
Avenge the Heart by Michele G. Miller
Curse the Night by R.K. Ryals (August 2018)
Blood & Iron by Amy Hale (September 2018)

More books releasing on a monthly basis.

Stay up to date at www.HavenwoodFalls.com

ALSO BY ANNALISA GRANT

For Donavan, Truman, and Claire.
So Much.

CHAPTER 1

The Greyhound bus jolted as it came to a stop, then hissed before the driver opened the door. Ivy Rapha wasn't the only one stretching and cracking her neck to either side. The bus was making a scheduled stop in Montrose, Colorado, two and a half hours into a five hour journey to Grand Junction. Ivy grabbed the only item she had—a backpack she hastily threw together before slipping out of the RV she shared with her parents—and stepped off the bus. She regretted not bringing her guitar. Her father kept it under the bed in their room, and there was no way Ivy could risk getting caught escaping. She would miss playing and singing, but music would always be there, even if she had to put it on hold while she made a new life for herself.

Ivy was glad the bus hadn't been full. In fact, it was quite near empty with only twenty passengers. It meant she didn't have to sit next to a stranger and field questions about why a young girl was traveling on a bus by herself at three in the morning, and then explain why eighteen years old wasn't so young. Being homeschooled, she had already graduated from high school, and for all they knew, she was on her way to some tiny college somewhere.

The bell above the door to the diner dinged, and Ivy found a seat at the counter.

"Hey, sweetheart. What can I get you?" The woman before her looked like she had walked straight out of a TV sitcom. Her pink waitress uniform had white, scalloped trim on the sleeves and collar, and her dirty blond hair was twisted up in a beehive. She had a pencil stuck behind her ear, which she pulled out to write down Ivy's order on the receipt pad in her hand. To top it off, her nametag actually read "Flo."

"Oh, uh, I don't know," Ivy stuttered. She pulled the menu from between the ketchup and mustard bottles and looked over it quickly. "I guess I'll just have a cheeseburger and fries. And a Coke?"

"Comin' right up!" Flo jotted down the order and then ripped the page from the pad, sticking it in a circular device hanging in the open window to the kitchen. "Cheeseburger and fries, Sam!" Then she visited the other guests around the diner and took their orders. That's when Ivy noticed that Flo was the only waitress there. Being that it was five-thirty in the morning, it didn't strike her as odd.

Ivy opened her backpack and pulled out a newspaper clipping. She read the caption under the photo to herself. *Woman dies in horrific accident just days after claiming she was healed of cancer.* She clenched her jaw and shoved the clipping back inside.

"Here you go, darlin'," Flo said, putting Ivy's plate in front of her.

"That was fast."

"It's not like we're slammed in here," she laughed.

Ivy let out a breathy laugh. "I guess not."

Keeping her eyes down, she picked up the ketchup bottle and squirted it over her fries. Then she removed the top of the bun and put a swirl of ketchup there, too.

Flo watched her for a minute, cocking her head to the side before she spoke. "You okay, sweetie? I mean, you're travelin' out here all by yourself . . ."

Ivy didn't look up. "I'm fine." Feeling her stare, Ivy lifted her eyes to Flo's. Now it was her turn to cock her head. There was something in Flo's eyes that drew Ivy in. Her gaze was warm and friendly, even motherly, and it calmed Ivy's nervous heart. "Actually . . ."

Flo smiled. "That's what I thought. I've seen a hundred girls like you come through here. I know a weary soul when I see one," she said. She crossed her arms and leaned her hip against the counter. "Tell Flo all about it."

Ivy was not going to tell Flo *all* about it, but she certainly felt compelled to get something off her chest.

"I wasn't in a very good situation with my parents. They were . . . not good people. I had to get out of there for my own safety and sanity." Ivy paused. "It sounds dumb, but I really need to . . . find myself."

"Sounds smart to me," Flo offered. "So where you headed?"

"My ticket is for Grand Junction, but that's just because it was the first bus out of Gunnison. The first bus out could have been to Neptune, and I would have taken it," Ivy said.

Flo nodded and pulled a folded piece of paper from her pocket. "Well," she began, "since you're not particular about where you're going . . ." She handed the paper to Ivy. "Folks seem to like this place a lot. Might be a good place to figure some things out."

Ivy took the paper. The words, "Visit Pole Creek Mountain," were splashed across the top with information at the bottom about the Rio Grande National Forest's hunting, fishing, and hiking adventures. Ivy smiled politely, set the paper down next to her plate, and took a bite of her burger. When she casually glanced at the flyer again, it was a completely different ad. "Visit Havenwood Falls!" were now the words across the top. Shuttle times from Montrose were listed below a scenic picture of the quaint town. Ivy blinked several times, and rubbed her eyes with the back of her burger-free hand. When the image didn't change back, she turned to the man seated at the table behind her.

"Excuse me," she said. "Can you tell me what this says?"

The man furrowed his brow, but obliged her. "Visit Pole Creek Mountain."

Ivy looked at the paper with the man. She squeezed her eyes shut tightly and then looked again. "Visit Havenwood Falls!"

"Um . . . thanks," she said.

All Ivy could think was that the intensity of her situation had finally caught up with her, affecting proper functioning of her mind. *Rest. I just need some rest,* she thought. *And food.* Ivy turned back to her plate and ate. She flipped the flyer over so there would be nothing to distract her from the nourishment her body so clearly needed. When she finished, Ivy took the ticket Flo had put in front of her, pulled enough money to cover her meal and a tip out of her bag, and tucked it under the edge of the plate. Then she slung her backpack over her shoulder and headed to the restroom. She closed and rubbed her green eyes, willing to wake them up enough to see clearly. Then she tied her long red hair back in a low ponytail and splashed some cool water on her face. When she returned a few moments later, the diner was empty and the Greyhound bus was nowhere to be seen.

"What the . . . ? They didn't wait for me?"

"The Greyhound waits for no man . . . or woman." An older, kind-looking African American man whom Ivy hadn't seen before stood at a table in the middle of the diner. He picked up dishes and stacked them in the bin in front of him. Ivy read his nametag: Brad. *Brad?* Seemed an odd name for an old, African American man, so she was sure she would have remembered seeing him earlier.

"Is Flo around?" Ivy asked the man.

"No one here but us chickens," Brad laughed.

Ivy furrowed her brow. She was about to peek her head into the kitchen when a bus pulled up. Not a Greyhound bus, but a bus just the same. The whole vehicle was an advertisement for the place only she had seen on the flyer from Flo. From the display, Havenwood Falls looked like a beautiful, quaint, and peaceful town. Ivy's stomach fluttered. Peaceful. That was exactly what she needed right now. A place where no one would know her or what she could do.

She didn't want to leave without saying goodbye or thank you to Flo, but by looking at the shuttle schedule on the flyer, Ivy knew that if she didn't catch this one, it'd be a long wait before the next one would arrive. She moved to the door and opened it, the bell above ringing out. When Flo didn't appear, Ivy did the only thing she could.

"Thanks, Flo!" The door closed behind her, and Ivy jogged to the bus.

BRAD WATCHED as she found a seat and the shuttle pulled away, and then smiled.

"You're welcome, darlin'."

CHAPTER 2

*T*he shuttle wound through the mountains, taking exits and turning onto streets that seemed to appear out of nowhere. Ivy's stomach grew queasy as she watched out the window. At least no one but the bus driver would see if she threw up. She was the only passenger. The bus driver, a pudgy woman with black, wiry hair, cast more than one stink-eyed glance at Ivy in the rearview mirror. Ivy wondered if she was concerned about an imminent cleanup in the aisle.

Two hours later, with the sun peeking over the mountains, Ivy arrived in picturesque Havenwood Falls. The town seemed to center around a common area with lush green grass, a gazebo, and a fountain. City Hall, the police station, shops, and even a charming inn lined the main streets. It was everything Ivy needed it to be.

The bus stopped, and Ivy moved to the front.

"Sure are a lot of people around for so early on a Saturday morning," she said to the driver.

"They're all probably headed to the Havenwood Falls Farmers' Market." The woman's gravelly voice caught Ivy off guard. She turned to look at her and felt terribly for thinking her hook nose made her look like a witch. Then she caught a glimpse of her nametag: Agatha. *Well, that seems unfortunate.*

"You should check it out. Lots of goodies to find there, my dear," Agatha continued.

"Yeah . . . sure. Sounds fun." Ivy stepped off the bus and spun around. "Oh! I forgot to ask how much I owed you."

"No charge, dear. All part of the hospitality of Havenwood Falls." She smiled, revealing an oddly perfect set of teeth. "Enjoy your stay!" The door closed, and Agatha drove off.

Ivy took a deep breath and adjusted her backpack. She surveyed the area, not sure where to start, but took Agatha's suggestion and followed the crowd to the farmers' market. No one seemed to pay much attention to Ivy. She simply flowed into the stream of people and soon found her way to Cook's Corner Park. Tables lined the perimeter of the park, where townspeople were selling various and sundry items. Some had fruits or vegetables. And there was a booth with the most beautiful flowers Ivy had ever seen. *Fairy Tale Florists. How cute.* And, because there's always at least one at a festival or farmers' market, there were tables filled with candles, incense, lotions, and potions. *Howe's Herbal Shoppe. Not too hard to guess what you're selling here in the Colorado mountains.* Ivy let out a breathy chuckle.

"Try some of my lotion, dear? The scent will drive the boys wild," a woman who strangely resembled Agatha called out to her.

"No, thank you," Ivy answered politely. She wandered by the tables, noticing the artistry of crafts like carved hiking sticks and dream catchers. And even sampled some of the most delicious rye bread she'd ever tasted.

Her feet and heart stopped when she came to the back corner of the park. There, across the street, was a cemetery. Ivy couldn't help herself. She crossed the way and stood at the gate, swallowing hard. She wondered how many of those buried there had met their demise in an instant, and how many had battled an illness that stole their final breaths slowly.

And she wondered how many of them she could have saved.

She was about to take a step into the cemetery when her hands began to tingle and grow warm. Ivy looked round. They grew hotter, and she knew that whoever needed her help was drawing closer. She lifted her palms, now glowing bright white. Ivy stepped back toward the farmers' market, but her hands began to cool, the sign that she was moving farther away from the subject. Just as Ivy spun back around, a young boy of about fifteen limped from out of the woods edging the cemetery, soaking wet. Not until he stumbled closer did she see the cuts and bruises on his face and just how tattered his clothes were.

"Hey!" Ivy called out. "Are you okay?"

Her hands burned and glowed hotter than ever before. The boy looked up at her and stopped, furrowing his brow.

"I'm fine," he panted.

"Here, let me help you." Before the boy could accept or reject her offer, Ivy was next to him. She draped his arm around her shoulder and slid hers around his waist. With one hand on his wrist and the other on his hip, all she had to do was wait. When the boy stopped in his tracks, she knew it was working.

"What . . . what are you doing to me?" he growled.

"I . . . nothing . . . just . . ."

He pushed Ivy away, sending her sailing six feet to his side and slamming her into the fence around the cemetery.

"Weston!" a man's voice cried out.

A dark-haired man who had to be at least six feet tall came barreling toward them. Following close behind him was a woman who Ivy thought looked like she could bake you the most amazing apple pie and then kick your ass right after.

"Dad! Mom!"

"What do you think you're doing?" the woman barked. "You had us worried sick!" She grabbed Weston's arm and yanked him forward.

"Wait!" Ivy called. "He's hurt."

The three turned around to find Ivy walking toward them. She had a slight limp, but the injury within her resolved itself with each step. By the time she reached them near the intersection, she was completely fine.

"And you are?" his father asked.

"I'm Ivy . . . Rapha. Ivy Rapha. I'm just visiting."

"She's more than just visiting, Dad," Weston said. "When she put her arm around me . . . something happened."

"What are you talking about?" Weston's mother stepped forward, her eyes boring into Ivy's before she turned her attention to her son.

"My whole body got hot. But my cuts and bruises, my cracked ribs," he looked at Ivy. "They burned like they were on fire."

Ivy's eyes grew wide. Never in all the times she had healed someone had they experienced such a profound reaction. Maybe a tingling sensation, at most, but nothing like what Weston described.

"Your hands," Weston's father observed.

Ivy lifted her still-glowing hands in front of her. "You can see that?"

"Of course we can see it." A smooth male voice called out from behind Weston's family.

The group turned to see who had joined them. Stepping off the curb and into the intersection was a dark-haired, broad-shouldered guy whose height matched that of Weston and his father. Dressed in dark jeans and a fitted maroon T-shirt, he looked to be about Ivy's age, maybe a year or two older.

"Justus Abbadon," Weston's mother said with disgust. "Should have known you had something to do with this."

"Looks like the girl was just trying to do you a favor," Justus said.

"We don't want anything from you, especially the way your family does *favors*."

The family started to leave with a still-injured Weston.

"Hey! I don't know him. I just got here and . . . really, I was trying to help," Ivy offered.

"Next time, ask someone if they want your help before you go setting fire to their insides." Weston's father tilted his chin down and set his eyes on Ivy. For just a moment, she could swear he was actually growling. They walked away, leaving Ivy shaking from the confusion burning inside her.

Ivy moved past Justus to the cemetery gate and picked up her backpack, then sat on the curb. What had just happened? They could see her hands glowing, and Weston's body burned with intensity as it tried to heal. Ivy didn't know which was more concerning. She replayed the event back in her mind. By the time she got to the end, one thing stuck out to her more than anything: her ability wasn't alarming to any of them.

What is this place?

Justus sat on the curb next to her and offered his hand. "I'm Justus—"

"Abbadon. Yeah, I picked up on that," Ivy said sharply. She studied him for a moment. Who was this guy who was cool, calm, and collected in the face of people who clearly wanted nothing to do with him? Weston's family didn't seem to trust him, but he had come to Ivy's aid, and for that, she was grateful. "Sorry." She shook his still-extended hand. "I'm Ivy Rapha."

"Welcome to Havenwood Falls, Ivy Rapha." He smiled.

Ivy made a hard line with her lips. She had been feeling quite welcomed until she was scolded for attempting to help someone.

"Thanks." Ivy thought for a moment. "Why were they so angry with me?"

"The Blaekthorns are very protective of their young."

"Their *young*?" Ivy's brows knit together at the peculiar term.

Justus tilted his head, the corner of his mouth lifting just slightly. "What are you?"

"What do you mean?" Ivy was even more confused now.

"I mean you obviously have some kind of supernatural power—" Justus bolted up and took three long strides away from Ivy. He turned and faced her with wide eyes. "Weston was hurt. Your hands . . ." He closed his eyes and let out a defeated sigh. "You're an angel."

Ivy stood quickly. "What? No! I'm not an angel. I'm not anything. I'm . . . just a girl." Justus ran his hand down his face and let out a long breath. "Why would you think I'm an angel? Not that they exist."

Justus laughed. The smile that had been creeping on his face erupted. "You have no idea where you are, do you? Wait. Better than that: you have no idea how you ended up here. Am I right?"

Ivy pulled the flyer Flo had given her slowly from her back pocket and unfolded it.

"When the woman at the diner first handed it to me, it said something entirely different. As soon as she walked away," she extended the paper to Justus, "it changed to this."

Justus took the paper and shook his head. "This damn place." He handed the flyer back to Ivy. "Well . . . you're here now. So we might as well get you registered."

"What?"

"The Court of the Sun and the Moon will want to see you right away." He looked at his watch. "It's still early, and with it being Saturday, they might have to call a special session."

"Thanks for the help back there, but I don't know you. I'm not going anywhere with you," she protested. If Ivy had learned anything from her parents, it was that you can't judge a book by its cover. Justus's cover was pretty hot, but he appeared out of nowhere and now he wanted Ivy to follow him like a lost puppy. No. If she was going to write the pages of her new life story, she would have to be smart.

"Suit yourself." Justus turned and walked back toward the farmers' market.

But . . .

Ivy stood there staring at the mysterious flyer in her hand. Justus's response to her explanation of it made it sound like she wasn't the first person to be magically lured to Havenwood Falls. Ivy sighed. The easiest thing would be to take the next shuttle back to Montrose and then go on to Grand Junction like she had planned. But, Grand Junction wasn't really her plan. Away from her parents to figure out her life was her plan. Whatever the reason, Ivy now found herself in the middle of a town where people could see and not be surprised by her ability. As much as she didn't like it, Justus Abbadon might actually have some answers for her.

"Hey!" she called out.

Justus turned around with a smirk plastered on his face.

"Change your mind?"

Ivy set her jaw, already regretting what she was about to say.

"If I go with you, will you answer my questions?"

"Seems like a fair trade," he said.

"Good." Ivy met Justus where he stood and then walked next to him, his long legs making it hard for her to keep up. "Who are the Blaekthorns? Who are you? And what is this hippie moon and sun court you're taking me to?"

Justus looked at her with that same crooked smile still on his face.

"Court of the Sun and the Moon. The Blaekthorns are shifters. Wolves to be exact. I'm a demon. And the Court is the true governing body of Havenwood Falls. All supernatural beings have to register with them so they know who, and what, is in town. Any other questions?" Ivy opened her mouth to speak, but nothing came out. "Well, I'm sure you'll think of a few more as soon as your brain has the slightest grasp of what's going on. In the meantime, I have one question for you: how do you feel about tattoos?"

CHAPTER 3

*I*vy walked alongside Justus back through the farmers' market, down the street, and to the town square. The place was teeming with people whom Ivy now knew were more than they appeared to be. But, in all fairness, so was she. Still, being in a town filled with people like her was unsettling. No. *Unsettling* wasn't the best word choice. She was freaking out.

"So you've seen Town Square Park," he said offhandedly. "The shuttle would have dropped you off somewhere around here . . ."

"Can we stop for a second?" Ivy dug her heels in on the corner in front of the fire station. "I appreciate the tour guide routine, but there's a lot of *holy crap* that I need to understand right now."

"You don't need to freak out, Ivy," Justus said.

"I'm not freaking out," she lied. "But if I were," she leaned her head in and lowered her voice, "it would be because you said you were a demon."

Justus looked around. "You don't need to whisper," he said. "Anyone who isn't supposed to know about us won't even be able to register the word demon with regard to my identity."

"Wha—"

Justus turned to an older woman walking toward them. "Good morning, Mrs. Jenkins. Did you know that I'm a demon?"

"Hello, Justus. Yes, it *is* a gorgeous day!"

They tilted their heads to each other, and Mrs. Jenkins continued on her way.

He turned back to Ivy, whose mouth was agape, and shoved his hands into his pockets. "Actually, scratch that. We're not supposed to talk about the town's secrets out in the open. So, if you could keep that one to yourself, that'd be great."

Ivy was too busy trying to decide if she was dreaming or not to respond.

"How did she not understand you?"

Now it was Justus leaning his head in and lowering his voice. "It's a little trick demons can do to make sure people hear what we want them to. Mrs. Jenkins and I go way back."

"Oh." Ivy's wide eyes didn't hide her bewilderment.

"It's a lot to take in. Let's just get you registered, and then I promise I'll answer anything you want to know."

"I'm not planning on staying here very long . . . especially not now. Why do I need to register with this Court of the, uh . . ."

"Court of the Sun and the Moon." Justus chuckled. "I already told you. They govern the town, and they have to know who's here."

Justus led Ivy around the corner behind City Hall and came to a metal door with a sun and moon symbol embossed into it. They entered and took the steps down into the basement. The hall they walked seemed to extend far beyond the depth of the building itself when they reached a door. Justus opened it without hesitation and stood to the side to let Ivy in first.

"I swear to God, if you kill me, I will haunt you for the rest of your unnatural life."

"You're going to fit in quite nicely here."

In the back corner of a large room similar to a court room was a desk with a credenza behind it and doors on either side that Ivy assumed led to other offices. Sitting with her feet propped up on the desk and crossed at the ankles was a girl in her mid-twenties, with light brown hair, black-framed glasses, a diamond stone in her nose, and tattoos—lots of them—on her arms. When she spoke, she didn't look up from the magazine she was reading.

"I thought I smelled smoke," she said.

"Nice to see you, too, Addie," Justus replied.

Addie raised her head and gave Ivy the once over. "What can I help you with?"

"She's just arrived in town and needs to register."

"Since when did Justus Abbadon start caring about the laws of the Court?" Addie scoffed as she stood. She opened the drawer to her right and pulled something from it Ivy couldn't immediately identify.

"I'm a law-abiding citizen," he said with a crooked grin.

"What you are is a loophole-abiding citizen," she sneered. Addie moved to the front of the desk and leaned against the edge. "All your kind are."

Justus looked down and shuffled his feet. "I found her near the cemetery as Weston Blaekthorn was coming out. Barney and Lydia weren't too happy with her, so I stepped in before someone got ripped to shreds."

"And why would they want to rip you to shreds?" Addie asked Ivy.

Ivy swallowed hard, clenching her nervous jaw. "He was injured and I tried to . . . heal him," she said softly.

"So you're an angel? Or maybe fae?" Addie drew her attention to Justus, raising her brow.

"She's not an angel," Justus said. He looked at Ivy. "I don't think she's sure what she is."

"Let me guess—you're going to help her figure that out."

Justus shook his head and moved to the door. "I'll wait for you outside."

Ivy had already learned there were demons and shifters in Havenwood Falls, so she was naturally curious as to what Addie could be. She didn't seem to care much for Justus either, but . . . Her stomach churned, realizing she didn't know if Justus's *friendly neighborhood tour guide* routine wasn't just an elaborate scheme to get her down to the basement where Addie would then do whatever demons did to people. Having spent nearly her whole life traveling with her fanatically fake religious parents, she had learned there was a myriad of things demons could do to someone, including, but not limited to: stealing your soul, blinding you, taking over your body, making you speak a different language, causing you to become mute, making you uncontrollably slutty, or killing you.

Yep. Freaking out.

"What's your name?" Addie asked.

"Ivy."

"How long are you planning on staying in our little town, Ivy?"

"I . . . I don't know. To be honest, I'm not even sure how I ended up here."

Addie sighed. "Sounds about right." She moved back behind the desk and picked up what she had taken from the drawer earlier. "Well . . . I don't know how you got here either. What I do know is that no one ends up in Havenwood Falls by accident. So if you're planning on sticking around, you've gotta follow the rules." Addie pulled a paper from the other side drawer of the desk and set it in front of Ivy. "The first one is this. Just fill it in and sign it."

Ivy looked over the form. It was pretty standard except for one part.

"*Species?* Um . . . human?"

"We're about to find that out." Addie pulled a pushpin from the desk and removed it from the tiny pouch it was sealed in. "First things first. Hold out your hand."

"What's this for?"

"This is how I find out exactly what kind of supernatural being you are."

"I'm not a *supernatural being*. I'm just—"

"You're just someone who has the power to heal people. You don't think that's supernatural?" Addie said. Ivy lowered her eyes and filled her lungs. She let it out slowly as she tried to calm her nerves. "Hey." Addie put her hand on Ivy's arm. "I don't know your story, but it sounds like all this is pretty new to you. Whatever the reason you have this ability, it's an important part of you now. Don't be scared of it." Addie smiled softly.

Ivy nodded and held out her hand. Addie pricked her finger and squeezed a few drops onto a petri dish Ivy hadn't seen her get. As soon as she had collected what she needed, Addie covered the dish and left the room.

Ivy stood there alone, hearing only the sound of her heart pumping blood at a rapid pace like a train through her ears. She looked at the door and wondered if she should just leave. Did she want to know what she was? Yes, of course she did. The power to heal had come on her unexpectedly just six months ago. Suddenly she was filled with hope that she would finally have some answers that might lead to figuring out where this power came from.

Addie returned with the petri dish in her hand and a look of confusion on her face.

"Well?" Ivy posed.

"Well . . . I've seen my fair share of hybrids, half-bloods, full-bloods, witches, warlocks, angels, and demons, but you, my new friend, are something altogether different. I've only seen this a few times but you are, mostly, human."

Ivy's heart sank. "I thought . . . I don't know what I thought."

"I said *mostly*. Don't you want to know what that tiny amount of *other* is?"

"Yes. No. I don't know." She held Addie's eyes with her own. "I'm scared."

Addie softened her edges and let a sweet smile cover her face.

"No need to be scared. You might even find it interesting," she said. "It's only a trace amount, but it's a hybrid of angel and fae—or faerie, as you'd know it."

"How is that possible?"

"You ever wish for anything?" Addie crossed her arms.

Ivy searched her memories. The first things that came to mind were birthday wishes, but having never received the pony of her dreams, she was certain those weren't the type of wishes that were magically granted. Nor were the kind that she had blurted out at her parents like, "I wish you would just leave me alone!" If only. Suddenly it hit her.

"Oh my god. I think I know, but . . . it can't be." She covered her mouth.

"You're doubting the origin of your ability, but not the ability itself?"

"I guess that doesn't make any sense, does it?"

Addie pulled a chair from the side of the room and placed it next to the desk. She indicated for Ivy to sit. "In my job with the Court, I've seen and heard it all. It may take you a while to reconcile all this. The good news is that you seem to be doing okay with your power. But, if I can offer you a little advice: do your best to hold back. Not all supernaturals will appreciate your abilities." Addie held up a thick, metal pen-type device and grinned. "Now for the best part."

"What is that?"

"It's a tattoo machine."

"I really have to get a tattoo? I thought he was joking."

"If you want to stay here you do." There was no change in the intonation of her voice, no manipulative intent, like Ivy thought she had heard in Justus's.

"Why a tattoo?"

"It's how all supernaturals, whether you're planning on staying a week or forever, register with the Court of the Sun and the Moon. There are rules to being in Havenwood Falls, and the tattoo is part of how we know who is and isn't abiding by them."

Ivy thought about it for a minute longer than Addie looked like she was willing to wait. She didn't know how long she wanted to stay. But she also wasn't sure if she wanted to leave either.

"What if I don't want to stay?"

"Well, you can leave anytime you want, but you'll forget all about Havenwood Falls and your time here," Addie told her. "You'll try to tell someone about it, but then sound like an idiot because you can't remember anything more than the mountains and being somewhere in Colorado. It's part of the magic that protects us from being discovered.

But, like I said, you can leave whenever you want. In the meantime, you gotta get tatted up."

"Um . . . okay."

Addie placed her other hand on the back of the device that held the ink. She closed her eyes for a moment and gave Ivy a slight smile.

"I've just infused the ink with magic specially created so you can exist safely in Havenwood Falls," she explained.

"What do you mean *safely?*"

"Just that the Court can monitor you and make sure you're abiding by the rules. One of the most important rules is protecting the secret, and that means we don't talk about the magical part of Havenwood Falls with *anyone* who isn't a supe." Addie set her gaze on Ivy. "This is a very important rule, Ivy."

"I got it." Ivy nodded, recalling Justus's request that she not tell anyone about his exchange with Mrs. Jenkins.

"Now, what kind of a tattoo do you want, and where are we putting it?"

Ivy twisted her mouth. "A treble clef." She turned her palm up. "Here, on the inside of my wrist."

Addie dipped her chin and got to work. Ivy thought that maybe she would want to see a picture or something, but if Addie had magic to infuse the ink, tattooing a treble clef freehand shouldn't have been a problem. Ivy waited for her wrist to burn or sting, but the short, fifteen-minute experience was a breeze.

When Addie was done, she held her hand over the tattoo and closed her eyes again.

"You're good to go," she said.

Ivy examined her tattoo and smiled. "I never thought I'd have one of these."

"Enjoy it while it lasts." Addie put the machine away and opened her magazine.

"It's only temporary?"

"It'll last as long as you stay in Havenwood Falls. If you leave, once you reach the limits of the memory ward on the town, the tattoo will disappear, and you'll forget this place ever existed. If you decide to become a resident, the rules change. You'll learn those if and when that happens."

"Oh." Ivy added that whole scenario to the list of questions she had about this mysterious town. She stood and moved to the door.

"You got a place to stay?" Addie asked.

"I hadn't gotten that far. Any cheap places to stay around here?"

"This is a Colorado ski town. Nothing is cheap. Go see Michaela at the Whisper Falls Inn. Tell her I sent you. She'll cut you a deal."

"Thanks, Addie. I appreciate your help." Ivy opened the door, but turned around to address Addie again. "If you don't mind me asking. What, um . . . what are you?"

"I'm the best thing of all. A witch," she said with a wink.

CHAPTER 4

S till shaken, Ivy walked back down the long corridor, up the stairs, and outside, where she took a deep breath of fresh mountain air. Justus was nowhere to be seen. Ivy wasn't sure if she was happy or disappointed. He had been so kind to her when he didn't have to be, but neither the Blaekthorns nor Addie hid their disgust with him. Maybe it would be better if he had taken off. If only she could crush that twinge of disappointment that was hanging on.

Ivy walked up the side of the building back to the sidewalk at the center of town in her quest for the Whisper Falls Inn. When she rounded the corner, Justus was leaning against a lamppost, his hands shoved in his pockets and his legs casually crossed at the ankles. She stopped and took him in for a moment. The sun was hitting his hair in such a way that he almost looked to have a halo. Ivy laughed at the irony.

"Hey," she called to him. "I didn't expect you to actually wait."

"Why? I told you I would." Justus motioned his head to the left and began walking, slower this time. Ivy's curious mind outweighed her hesitant feet, and she met up with him, keeping in better stride this time.

"I don't know." Ivy shrugged. "Maybe I'm waiting for you to be the big jerk everyone seems to think you are."

Justus stopped and turned to Ivy. "Do *you* think I'm a jerk?

"So far . . . no."

"Then why can't that be enough?"

Justus resumed his pace and Ivy followed. They crossed at the corner and walked down the sidewalk on Eighth Street. It was a beautiful summer day, and people were in the town square playing with their kids and throwing Frisbees with their dogs. They crossed again and walked past a bar and a bookstore before Justus stopped.

"You hungry? They've got a killer blueberry scone, and the coffee's pretty decent."

Ivy looked at the sign in the window. *Coffee Haven.* It had been quite a morning, and Ivy was sure the adrenaline rush from earlier had worked off that burger and fries from the diner in Montrose.

"Coffee would be great," she answered. "And I'm going to trust you on that blueberry scone." Ivy smiled.

Justus held the door for her, and they walked in. With old wooden floors and a long marble counter, it was clear the place had been converted from its original existence into the now bustling coffee shop. Justus found a small table near the back. Ivy told him how she liked her coffee and waited while he placed their order.

Ivy looked around the shop and wondered what the supernatural-to-just-natural ratio was. Then she realized that she had increased the supernatural number by a factor of one just by walking in. How many in there were witches like Addie or shifters like the Blaekthorns or demons like Justus?

"Here you go." Justus placed a plate with two blueberry scones between them and then darted back to the counter to pick up their coffees and an extra plate.

"The way people have been acting, I'm surprised they served you," Ivy said.

"Yeah, well, Harlow likes me. Despite what the rest of the Luna Coven thinks." Justus took a bit of scone and then a sip of his coffee.

"What's the Luna Coven?"

"That's the coven Addie's family belongs to," he told her. "They pretty much run this town. Along with the Court, of course." Ivy nodded as she tried to digest more weird information about this place. "Are you okay? You looked pretty shaken when you came out of City Hall."

"I don't know." She was being honest. "Can anyone be okay finding out they have trace amounts of angel and faerie in them?" Ivy broke off a piece of the scone and popped it in her mouth. Justus had *not* oversold the pastry.

"So you *are* an angel?" Justus lowered his voice and his eyes.

"I guess. Technically. But then I'm *technically* a faerie, too." Ivy took note of Justus's dismay. "What's wrong?"

He looked at her as if she should know. "Angels. Demons. They don't mix well."

"I'm not that kind of angel, if you can even call me that. Addie said it was trace amounts. How does that even work?"

Justus furrowed his brow. "You really don't know how you got this power of yours?"

Ivy shook her head. "No. Well, I didn't until Addie asked me a similar question. Now I'm just speculating."

"What do you think happened?"

"It's a long story."

Justus fixed his eyes on Ivy's. They were soft and kind and nothing like that of a demon's. "I've got all day."

Ivy put her fingertips to her mouth and looked away. She wasn't sure if she should tell Justus. She had just met him, and there was no indication from anyone else that he was trustworthy. No indication except the fact that he had helped her when he didn't have to. He could have left the Blaekthorns to deal with her, but he stepped in, knowing how they felt about him. He took a risk on her.

Justus put his scone down. "I know that look. I just told you that demons and angels don't mix well, but I'm still here," he said. Disappointment coated his words.

Ivy let out a long breath, releasing any anxiety she had about revealing the truth of her transgressions. Despite how Ivy had seen Justus treated, there was something about him that put her at ease.

"Well," she began, "I've spent my whole life traveling around the country with my parents in an RV. We went from town to town, and they set up big tent revivals. I'd play my guitar and sing for the crowd and then my dad would get up and do his thing, preaching and healing people. Well, not really healing people. See, that was their thing . . . their scam. They would find people in a town nearby and hire them to come to the next town and claim they were sick. Some even showed up in wheelchairs. Then my dad would shout something crazy, and they'd jump up from the chair, or claim they could feel a rush of electricity through their body and they just *knew* it was the cancer leaving them.

"So then they'd set up these healing sessions the next night where people would come and *donate* a hundred dollars to their *ministry*," Ivy made air quotations with her hands, "so they could be healed. They'd get a hundred people there. A hundred desperate people who I just stood by and watched get scammed."

"You can't take responsibility for what your parents did, Ivy. You were a kid and at their mercy."

"Maybe. But then this happened and . . ." Ivy stared at the palms of her hands.

"What did happen?"

Ivy closed her eyes and remembered the days that led up to the moment her life changed forever. She swallowed the lump that had formed in her throat.

"We had a healing session one night. Part of my job was to chat people up as they waited in line. Tell them how great it was going to be. Keep their hopes up. Take their money. This woman came through. Carla. I struck up a conversation with her, and she told me how she had pawned some family heirlooms to get the money for her session. Her family told her not to, but she was desperate. She was 40 years old and had stage four colon cancer. So, I refused to take her money. I figured my parents would never know. The woman would go through, Dad would do his thing, and she'd be on her way. She was going to die anyway. I just couldn't take her money.

"But, Dad found out somehow and refused to see her. She begged. I begged. But he spouted some crap about 'you would never ask your mechanic to fix your car for free' and 'isn't God more worthy than your mechanic?' I told her how sorry I was and that she should try to get her things back from the pawnshop.

"There were so many people there that first night that we ended up staying another two days. One of Carla's friends came through on the last night. Becky told me that Carla had taken a turn for the worse and was in the hospital. So, after the session, I asked Carla's friend to take me to her. It was late, but Becky convinced the nurse that I was Carla's daughter and had just arrived from out of town."

Ivy sighed and took a sip of her coffee. It was a bit cooler now. Her stomach fluttered as she recalled the next moments of her story. Justus sat there quietly, his attentive eyes locked on her. He didn't sip his coffee or take another bite of scone. Every ounce of him was focused on every word that left Ivy's lips.

"I sat down and took her hand in mine. She was so drugged up that she didn't even know I was there. I couldn't help but think of the countless people my dad had convinced he had healed, but who never got better. It made me sad to think that they probably blamed themselves for not having enough faith or worse, blamed God. Like He had anything to do with what my parents were doing. And I just remember putting my head on the fist of our hands, crying, and whispering that I wished I could really heal her."

"And that was it? That's when you got this power to heal?"

"When I asked Addie how I could be part angel and part faerie, she asked if I had ever made a wish. This is the only thing that makes any sense in this thing that doesn't even make sense."

"Did you heal Carla that night?" Justus asked.

Ivy's eyes dropped. "No. It wasn't until we hit the next town that I had any, uh, symptoms. I was going out to monitor the line, and my hands grew warm and started to glow. I was freaking out, but no one else could see it. The closer I moved to the line, the hotter they got. I pressed through the crowd to get out of the tent and in the process, grabbed hold of this man. I felt this . . . this . . . energy leave me, and I became completely drained. Like, I-couldn't-stand-up drained. But the next thing I know, he's shouting how he was blind in his left eye, but can see out of it now."

"What did your parents do?" he asked.

Ivy was sure Justus, being a demon, had seen and created his fair share of supernatural events, yet he seemed intrigued by Ivy's story, leaning in like he was anxiously awaiting the next details.

"First, my dad flipped. But my mom calmed him down and said this was the best thing that could ever happen, because now they could charge twice as much, if not more, for actual healings." Ivy let out a sad sigh. "So that's what we did. We went from town to town, and I took center stage at the healing sessions."

"That's messed up. And that's saying a lot, considering my family history."

"The worst part is that I found out some of the people I healed died just days or weeks later. This one woman in particular . . ." Ivy ran her hand down her scrunched face. "I mean . . . what was the point if they were just going to die anyway?"

"Everyone dies, Ivy. Well, every *human* dies."

Ivy thought for a minute. "Actually, maybe the *worst* part is that I went along with it. I never told my parents I didn't want to do it. So for six months, I was compliant in charging people exorbitant amounts of money to use a gift I had been given." She turned the cup around in her hands and steeled herself. "I turned eighteen two weeks ago and decided I'd had enough. I found out when we'd be in a town with a bus station and made a plan. I grabbed the cash box and snuck out in the middle of the night, walked three miles to the bus station, and bought a ticket for the next bus out. I didn't even care where it was going."

"And then you *mysteriously* ended up here, in Havenwood Falls." Justus smirked and shook his head.

"You say it like that happens a lot," Ivy said.

"Enough."

Ivy took a sip of her coffee and then broke off a piece of scone. She broke that piece in two and then continued to pick at the pieces between her fingers.

"Okay, that's enough about me." She let out a nervous laugh. "What's your deal? Why is Harlow the only person in this town who likes you?"

"It really has more to do with my family. Guilty by association and all. But . . ." He sighed. "You didn't escape your own family drama to hear about mine."

"Actually," Ivy said, "I think it might help to hear how jacked up other people's families are. I mean . . . my parents can't be the worst, can they?" Ivy's heart sank. In her mind, the answer to that question was a resounding yes. They were, in fact, the worst.

Justus laughed. "They are certainly *not* the worst."

"Your mom and dad can't be that bad," Ivy argued.

"It's just me and my dad," he said. "He runs a finance company—loans and investments—and to be honest, he's pretty shady."

Ivy bit her lip, pondering if she should speak her mind. "No offense, but demons don't exactly have a great reputation of being anything other than shady."

"I can't argue with that." Justus stood, signaling their get-to-know-me time was over. He held his arm out, and Ivy stood and walked ahead of him.

"So, where to now?" Justus asked, completely avoiding any further conversation about himself.

"Um . . . I guess I need a place to stay. Addie suggested I see someone named Michaela at the Whisper Falls Inn."

"Oh. Great. Vampires."

Ivy folded her arms and cocked her head to one side. "Is there anyone in this town you get along with?"

"It's a short list."

CHAPTER 5

*J*ustus walked Ivy down the block to Whisper Falls Inn, which sat at an angle on the corner facing Town Square Park. They got to the steps of the large, three-story Victorian-style manor when Justus stopped.

"I think I'm going to sit this one out," he told Ivy. "I mean . . . you don't really need me anymore anyway." He shoved his hands in his pockets and took two steps back.

"Oh, um . . . right," she stuttered. "Thanks for all your help. And for the coffee and the scone."

Justus nodded. "Sure. Well, maybe I'll see you around."

"Maybe." Ivy smiled and walked up the steps and onto the wraparound porch. She opened the door and entered the lobby. The front desk was to the left and an octagonal-shaped parlor was on the right. Seated behind the desk was a rail-thin girl whose eye roll said Ivy's existence was an inconvenience for her.

"Hi." Ivy smiled and clutched the straps of her backpack by her shoulders.

"Yeah?" the girl replied.

"Um . . . Addie told me to see Michaela about a room?"

Before the girl behind the desk could finish her annoyed sigh, a girl who looked to be in her early twenties appeared in the doorway to the back office. She smiled and stepped out.

"I'm Michaela," she said. "And you are?"

Relieved she didn't have to navigate the teen angst sitting before her, Ivy smiled back. "I'm Ivy Rapha. Addie said to see you about a room."

"Sure." Michaela nudged the girl out of the way. "This is my little sister Aurelia. She's this rude to everyone, so don't take it personally." Aurelia rolled her eyes again and went into the back office. Michaela clacked away at the computer. "You're in luck. I've got one room with a private bath left. It's a little more than the others, but we girls prefer our own space, right?"

"Right." Ivy laughed nervously. This place looked like a room with a private bath was going to be pricey. She had a few thousand dollars tucked away in her backpack. And, while it was a lot of money, Ivy didn't know how long she was going to have to make it stretch. "Addie also said that you'd cut me a good deal?"

Ivy wrung her hands. That's when Michaela's gaze dropped to the fresh tattoo on her wrist.

"How long are you planning on staying in Havenwood Falls?" Michaela asked.

"I'm not sure. I wasn't even planning on coming *to* Havenwood Falls."

"I know the feeling." Michaela chuckled and smiled. "Don't worry. Take a few days and once you have things figured out, we'll decide on a fair price."

Before Ivy could express her gratitude, Aurelia called from the back office.

"*Kaekae!* There's a guy on the phone about the ad for a singer in the restaurant!"

Michaela turned her annoyed face toward the office. "Take his number, and I'll call him back, Aurelia." She gave her attention to Ivy again. "Sorry about that."

"You're looking for a singer?"

"Yeah. Why? You suddenly know someone?"

"You're looking at her. But," Ivy's eyes dropped, "I had to leave my guitar behind."

Michaela cocked her head and considered Ivy. "Cecelia at the music store has some good used guitars. She's the owner, and I'm sure she can find something for you. As soon as you've got something, let me hear you, and I'll see about having you play a couple nights a week."

"That'd be great." A small smile crept onto Ivy's face, followed quickly by a yawn too big to stifle. "Excuse me."

Michaela made a few more clicks on the computer and then handed Ivy a key. "I know it's only ten in the morning, but it already looks like you could use a nap."

Ivy yawned again. "I guess so."

"Your room is at the top of the stairs. Second door on the left," Michaela told her. "And hey . . . I know what it's like. Discovering something about yourself that doesn't make any sense. If you want to talk . . ."

"That's really nice of you, Michaela. I think what I need most right now is to sleep."

Michaela nodded, and Ivy made her way up the stairs and to her room, which was decorated in a manner that suited the inn. The furniture was antique, and the bedding was soft and simple. There was a tufted chair in front of the window, a rocking chair in the corner, and a tall dresser on the wall next to the bathroom. Ivy put her backpack on the floor next to the window and fell onto the white, four-poster bed. Within seconds, she was fast asleep and dreaming. It was the most vivid dream Ivy had ever had. Unfortunately, it was about the life she was so desperately trying to leave behind.

Ivy stood at the front of a large crowd, her father shouting out from the side while her mother ushered the sick and infirm from the line up to her. After a few people passed through, Ivy's strength was nearly gone. But her mother brought one more to see her before Ivy could do no more. An old woman in a turn-of-the-century-style purple dress stood before her. She was short and plump with gray hair and beautiful gray eyes. She took Ivy by the shoulders and smiled. A warm rush of emotion flooded Ivy. It was like nothing she had ever felt before. She was calm. Happy. Peaceful.

"It's all going to be okay," the woman said. "You're not alone." The grandmotherly gaze of the woman's eyes into hers seemed to wipe away some of the pain Ivy had been carrying. She tried to speak, but as happens all too often in dreams, she had no voice.

Ivy woke with wet eyes. She sat up and pressed the hem of her shirt to her face, soaking up the tears and taking a long, cleansing breath. A creaking sound came from the corner of the room. When Ivy looked, she was startled to see the woman from her dream sitting in the rocking chair, smiling with her hands clasped beneath her chin.

"Oh, you are a lovely girl, aren't you?" she said to Ivy.

"What . . . Who . . . How . . ." Ivy stuttered. She was just happy to have a voice this time.

"Now, don't you fret, honey. I'm Luiza Petran, and this is my home. Well, it *was* like my home until . . ." She motioned to her body that wasn't quite solid, yet not completely transparent either. Ivy may have just discovered this mysterious town, but it didn't take a Ghostbuster to see that the woman before her was, indeed, a ghost. "Now it belongs to my niece, Michaela."

Ivy examined the woman rocking away in front of her. Just as she had in Ivy's dream, Madame Luiza's presence made her feel at ease.

"It's nice to meet you, Mrs. Petran," Ivy said.

"Oh, now, call me Madame Luiza, as everyone else does." The old woman smiled with such joy that Ivy couldn't help but mirror her expression.

"Okay, Madame Luiza," she said. "So, uh . . . you were totally just in my dream."

"I thought that might be an easier way for us to meet. I know all of this is very new to you, and having a ghost waiting for you when you woke may have filled you with a little fright."

Ivy was anything but afraid. "I just got here this morning, and already I've met a shifter, a demon, a witch, and a vampire. Meeting a ghost is really just icing on the strangest cake I've ever seen." She let out a breathy laugh. "I don't mean to sound rude, but is there a reason you're here?"

"I'm here to help you with the reason *you're* here, honey."

"And what is that?" Ivy wondered if Madame Luiza had been the one behind drawing her to Havenwood Falls.

Madame Luiza laughed. "Oh, I don't know that! I'm a ghost, not a clairvoyant! I'm just here to offer a little love and guidance as you figure things out."

"Oh." Ivy didn't hide her disappointment.

Madame Luiza stood and approached Ivy. When her hand landed on her shoulder, Ivy was surprised at how real it felt.

"How am I supposed to know why I'm here?" Ivy asked.

"Just follow your gut, honey. Your gut is never going to lie to you." Luiza smiled. "You'll know who you can and can't trust in the process."

Ivy thought of Justus. He'd been given the cold shoulder by nearly everyone they'd come in contact with that day. She didn't know what his father had done to them, or why they would assume Justus was just as guilty, but Ivy's gut told her that he was a good guy. How could her gut be right and a whole town be so wrong?

"Now," Madame Luiza continued, "you'd best be on your way to the music store. Michaela's been making some changes around here, and I think having a singer in the restaurant a few nights a week is a wonderful idea!" She clasped her hands beneath her grin. "Seems you've joined us in just the nick of time!"

"Thank you, Madame Luiza." Ivy sighed. "Will you be here when I get back?"

"Honey, I'm not going anywhere . . . ever." She laughed.

With that, Madame Luiza turned toward the door and walked through the wall next to it, out into the hallway.

Ivy opened her backpack and spread the few belongings she had brought with her on the bed: the necessary toiletries and underwear, two pairs of jeans, a few shirts, and a gray hoodie. It wasn't much to look at, but it was all hers.

After an almost baptismal shower, Ivy put the money she had taken from her parents on the bed, too. Then she separated it, finally counting all that was there: $4,750. Her bus ticket had been $150. She divided the bills into $500 increments and tucked them away in various places around the room for safekeeping. She took the last $250, folded it, and shoved it in her back pocket. Regardless of how long she would be there, if she was going to be working at the inn, she thought she might need something nicer to wear than what she had. And while she hoped to find a good used guitar for less than $50, there were no guarantees.

She opened the door and paused for a moment. Should she be using the money her parents had scammed off those poor people? Technically, Ivy had earned it. And, really, the main point was that her parents didn't have it. Ivy was using the money to start a new life away from the lies and deceit of her parents. She shook her head. It was too much to think about. Ivy wasn't going to look back. Her only objective was to understand her new powers and use them honestly.

CHAPTER 6

*I*vy locked the door and closed it behind her. On her way out, Michaela gave her directions to Havenwood Falls Music & More, which was just across the street and a few doors down.

The crowd in Town Square Park had dwindled down to almost nothing. And the mountains that surrounded the small town now shadowed the whole square. Ivy took the short walk to the music store and stepped inside. It was a small space, but seemed to be well stocked with instruments of all types. There was even a recording studio in the back. She found the wall of guitars and scanned the area to see if any of them were marked as used.

"Good afternoon." A petite woman with blond hair and blue eyes, who looked to be in her mid-twenties, appeared at Ivy's side. Ivy took note of her name tag: Cecelia. She also took note of the sadness in her eyes. It was the kind of look that could only come from a lost love. Ivy wished her power worked on healing broken hearts.

"You're the owner," Ivy said.

"Yes, ma'am," she said softly. She threaded her delicate fingers together in front of her.

"I'm Ivy. I'm looking for a used guitar. Michaela said she thought you might have one at a good price."

A sweet smile appeared on Cecelia's face as she studied Ivy. "I think I have just the thing for you." She turned and called to the back of the store. "Glenn, can you come here please?"

A guy about Ivy's age approached. He plastered on an eager smile and addressed Cecelia. "Did you need some help getting an instrument down?"

"Not this time, dear. My new friend Ivy is looking for a good used guitar. Could you get the cherry wood Martin from my office, please?"

"The Martin?"

"Yes. The Martin."

Glenn furrowed his brows, but then raised them as he acquiesced.

"You're new in this place," Cecelia said.

"It's that obvious?" Ivy laughed nervously. "I just arrived this morning."

"I mean you're *new* in *this* place." Cecelia covered her heart with her hand.

Ivy understood her meaning. "What?"

"We angels know our own kind," she said sweetly.

Ivy didn't want to tell her that she wasn't a full-blooded angel, or that she was part faerie. She assumed that the angel in Cecelia saw the angel in her. It was kind of nice, actually. Ivy had felt like a freak since she got her powers. It had only been a day, but just being in Havenwood Falls made Ivy feel a lot more normal than she had in a long time.

The bell rang above the door. Ivy turned to see Justus timidly walking toward her. He looked at Cecelia, seemingly unsure if he should come any closer. She smiled softly at him and nodded before stepping away.

"Hey," he said to Ivy, his confidence restored.

"Hey. What are you doing here?"

"I was just—"

"Here you go," Glenn said, returning with the guitar. He glowered at Justus when he saw him. "Justus," he sneered.

"Glenn." Contempt rolled smoothly off Justus's tongue. He

35

returned Glenn's stare before giving his attention back to Ivy. "I'll wait for you outside."

Ivy nodded.

"You should stay away from him," Glenn warned. "His family is no good."

"People keep saying that, but no one has yet given me an explanation." Ivy cocked an expectant eyebrow. "Is it just because they're—" Ivy caught herself before she broke the cardinal rule of being a supernatural being in Havenwood Falls.

"Is *wealthy* the word you're looking for?" Glenn scoffed. "I don't care how rich his family is. They're manipulative people who will do whatever it takes to get what they want, even if that means destroying everything in your whole life." Glenn clearly had some firsthand experience with Justus's family. "Just do yourself a favor and steer clear of the Abbadons."

"That's enough, Glenn." Cecelia returned and took the guitar from him. Glenn gave Ivy a small smile and walked away.

Cecelia put the strap over her head and let the guitar hang. She strummed the strings and tweaked the tuning knobs until it was just right. Then she handed the instrument to Ivy.

"Uh . . ." Ivy hesitated to take the guitar in her hands. "This is not a used guitar. I thought I'd misheard you when you said Martin. Even if this is used, I really can't afford it."

Cecelia pushed the guitar into Ivy's hands. "Play something for me."

Ivy's stomach churned. She was used to playing for hundreds of people at the rallies with her parents, not just one person. Although, she didn't imagine the restaurant at the inn would be filled with large crowds, so it was probably a good exercise that would help work the nerves out.

"Um, okay." Ivy lifted the strap over her head and strummed. It felt good to have an instrument in her arms. While she had exclusively played religious-type music at the rallies, Ivy's preferred style was old standards. She also liked to take current songs and put a retro spin on them. Ivy played a few bars of her take on a popular song, putting a smile on Cecelia's face.

"That was beautiful, Ivy. So beautiful that I can't stand the thought of you not playing *that* guitar. Consider it my gift to you." Ivy opened her mouth to speak, but Cecelia cut her off. "And don't even think of rejecting my offer."

"Are you sure?" Ivy asked as more of a protest. Cecelia only stared at her. "Okay. Wow. Thank you so much."

Cecelia helped her put it back in its soft case.

"Now, it seems there's a pretty hot guy waiting outside for you." She smirked.

"You don't have a problem with Justus?"

"I don't think anyone should be judged based on the sins of their fathers," she answered. She leaned in a little closer. "I also think that boy out there just might be the reason you're here."

Ivy looked out the store window. Justus leaned against a street lamp as he had earlier. Cool. Casual. It was beyond her what he could possibly have to do with her being in Havenwood Falls.

Justus turned when the bell above the door rang as Ivy exited. He gave her a small smile, which Ivy reciprocated. What was it about him that she just couldn't shake . . . besides the fact that he seemed to also not be able to shake her? Ivy was happy to hear Cecelia speak kindly of him, and she wondered if maybe she was right. Six months ago, Ivy would have scoffed at the idea of a town filled with people with supernatural powers and abilities. But now that she was one of them, nothing shocked her. She was standing there, part angel, in front of a demon. And while most of the town saw him as such, Ivy had yet to see anything of Justus Abbadon that resembled evil.

"You had a burning desire to buy a guitar?" Justus asked.

"You had a burning desire to come looking for me?" Ivy smirked.

"Touché." He nodded his head to the side, and Ivy took her cue to walk alongside him. "I was on my way to grab some pizza and saw you through the window. I thought you might want to join me."

Ivy's belly rumbled at the mere mention of food. Laughing, she placed her hand on her stomach. "Guess there's no getting out of this one, huh?"

"Great," Justus said. "Now your turn. What's up with the guitar?"

"Michaela is adding musicians a few nights a week in the restaurant at the inn. She said if I could get a guitar, then she'd hear me play and then maybe let me perform," she told him. "I hope she likes me, because it'll let me work off part of the cost of my stay if she does."

"I'm sure you're great."

The two walked toward the Whisper Falls Inn, but turned down Main Street on the Town Square Park side of the street. Then they took the path toward the fountain. Ivy opted to keep the guitar with her rather than drop it at the inn. It was an expensive instrument and Ivy wasn't ready to let it leave her sight. She also was pretty sure that she'd get caught up talking with Madame Luiza, and she didn't want to leave Justus hanging.

As they approached the fountain, a woman walking her dog got tangled up in the leash. Her body twisted and contorted uncontrollably until she fell. Ivy and Justus winced at the sight and immediately went to help. It took no time at all for Ivy's hands to begin to burn like fire and glow white hot. The woman on the ground looked up at them as they approached, crying for help. Ivy looked at Justus to ask silent permission to touch her, knowing as soon as she did, her healing powers would take over. After her experience with the Blaekthorns, Ivy feared angering another supe. Justus nodded, confirming that the woman was human. Not only would Ivy's help be better received, but the human woman wouldn't even know.

"Oh my gosh! Are you okay?" Ivy knelt down next to the woman, who was grabbing her arm. Ivy placed her hand on her back. The woman's breathing began to regulate, and her tears dried.

"Actually," the woman said, "I'm fine. I think I just got all rattled!" She laughed, and Justus helped her stand. Ivy, however, could not.

The woman thanked them and continued on her way. Justus sat next to Ivy on the grass.

"What happened?" He placed his hand on Ivy's back. Her body

was burning hot, and she was working to keep her head up. "Ivy! Are you—"

"I'm okay," she mumbled. "This is what happens anytime I heal someone. It drains me of . . . something. I don't know what." She laid her head on Justus's shoulder. He pulled her closer to him, and Ivy decided that she didn't care what anyone else in that town had to say. Demon or not, Justus Abbadon was a good man, and she was glad to know him. "You said something about pizza?"

"Are you still up for that?"

"Definitely. I'm even more famished now." Ivy sat up and wobbled a bit.

"I'm taking you back to the inn," Justus declared. "If you're that hungry, we can eat at the restaurant there."

"But . . . pizza," Ivy whined.

"No arguing, young lady." Justus raised Ivy to her feet with no effort at all. She wondered if he was just that strong or if that was a demon thing. She had so much to learn about this supernatural world.

Justus all but scooped her up in his arms and carried her back to the inn. His arm fit snugly around her waist as he helped her up the front steps. Aurelia gave him the stink eye when he entered, but she gave everyone the stink eye. When Michaela asked what happened, Justus told them briefly and that she needed to eat.

"I hope this isn't a game, Abbadon," Michaela said.

"It's not," Ivy told her. Michaela walked away after setting two menus in front of them.

"Ivy," Justus began, "what you did for that woman was great and all, but you're really not supposed to do that."

"Why not?"

"Just part of the rules here," he told her. "The Court can't have supes running around using their abilities on human townspeople."

"But I'm using it for good," Ivy argued. "And it's not like with Weston Blaekthorn. That woman didn't even know."

"Whether she knew or not isn't the issue. Someone else could use their powers for the opposite. So, they make it kind of an across the board rule. It'd have to be some pretty special circumstances for the Court not to reprimand you or worse, banish you from town."

"Oh." Ivy twisted her mouth. If that was the rule, Ivy foresaw a lot of hiding at the inn in her future.

The two spent the evening eating pasta primavera and Alaskan salmon and avoiding all conversation about what it meant that Ivy was part angel and that Justus was a demon. By the time they finished, Ivy was ready to pass out, but this time it was from a food coma. She thanked Justus and asked if she'd see him again tomorrow.

"I think I could find some time to squeeze you in," he joked. Ivy smiled. She pushed up on her toes and wrapped her arms around his neck. Justus's arms snaked around her waist, first hesitantly, then with a firm hold.

"Thank you for all your help today." She let out a small laugh. "Today. I've only been here a day. Weird." Ivy grabbed her new guitar and carried her worn-out body up the stairs and to her room.

JUSTUS EXITED to the porch with a satisfied grin spread across his face and jogged down the steps of the inn. His smile was quickly wiped away when he nearly slammed into the dark figure waiting for him at the end of the sidewalk.

"Justus," the man said.

"Father."

"So? Have you gathered all the information on the girl?"

CHAPTER 7

*A*t six foot five, Siler Abbadon towered over his six-one son. With jet-black hair and eyes that were so brown they were almost black, it was easy to see what Justus would look like inside of ten years. He was the reason people in town treated Justus so coldly. Siler was the sole proprietor of Abbadon Finance, a company that provided personal loans and investment services. While his investment practices weren't one hundred percent on the up and up, it was the personal loan side of the business that had built his less-than-respectable reputation.

"I'm working on it," Justus told him sharply.

"Pavan's boy, Tarun, said you had quite a conversation at Coffee Haven this morning. And then there was an incident at the fountain . . ." Demons were suspicious creatures in and of themselves, which made them suspicious of everyone . . . even each other.

"You're having one of your lackey's lackeys follow me?" Justus shoved his hands in his pockets and pushed past his father. He crossed Eleventh Street and continued along the sidewalk on Main. His father followed.

"I wouldn't have to if you would report back to me on your own."

Justus cleared his throat. "It all just happened this morning. You think she was going to spill everything to me in one meeting? And be lucky that I found her and not that idiot Tarun. She'd never tell him anything."

"It's true. You're better at compelling than anyone in our legion," Siler said. Justus stopped in front of Coffee Haven and took a deep breath. "You haven't compelled her, have you? I don't know why you refuse to use your natural abilities, son. They were given to you for a reason."

"This isn't a case where I need to use them. She . . . she trusts me."

Siler's hand gripped his son's shoulder. "Well then, what information do you have for me?"

"Not here." Justus jerked away, out of his father's hold, and found his way to Siler's Porsche Cayenne he mistakenly thought was discreetly parked behind the Havenwood Village Apartments.

The drive to their home in the elite Havenwood Heights neighborhood was silent. They pulled through the ornate double gate to the community and followed the roads to the very back of the development. Most of the homes there were owned by original families of Havenwood Falls. The Abbadons took ownership of this home one hundred years ago, after Siler's business finally yielded him the kind of money that demanded they have only the best. Had the founding families understood just what the small print of all Abbadon Finance contracts meant, they would have never been allowed to stay.

Siler pulled into the circular drive in front of their home, and they both got out. A butler with a robotic personality greeted them at the door, taking Siler's jacket. Father and son moved into the large sitting room, where a fire was already roaring in the fireplace. The outside temperature had dropped to close to forty-five degrees, but it didn't matter. A fire blazed in the Abbadon home 365 days a year.

Siler sat in a soft, wingback chair the color of blood. He lit a cigar, crossed his legs, and looked expectantly at his son.

Justus clenched his jaw before he spoke. "She's not what we thought she might be. She doesn't even know how she got the power to heal," he lied. Siler looked over his nose at his son. "She's not an angel." This was only a partial lie.

Siler stood and circled the chair, gripping the back with his bony fingers.

"That's all we needed to know. Isn't that good enough?" Justus said through his teeth.

"No. It's not." Siler stepped closer to his son. "She's a healer, but not an angel. That means we have no idea what the parameters are on her powers, if there even are any. If she begins healing the gravely ill—"

"She won't be allowed to," Justus argued.

"You never know what the Court will do," Siler countered. "You and I both know they allow certain people to practice their talents if it benefits them. If she's allowed to heal, we'll lose clients strapped by medical bills. More importantly, we'll lose their souls. Without their signed contracts, we'll have no legitimate access to their souls, and the Court will have us banished. Is that what you want?"

Justus shook his head.

"Is. That. What. You. Want?" Siler's reiteration demanded a vocal response.

"No."

"Good. Then ensure the longevity of our legion in Havenwood Falls by either finding out how we can take possession of her soul, or getting her out of town. Are we clear?"

"Fine."

"Where are your manners, son?"

Justus clenched his jaw. "Yes, sir."

"That's better." Siler took a deep breath and smiled. "It is your destiny, after all. You've graduated from that filthy school, and soon you'll stop showing signs of aging. It's time to follow in your father's footsteps and join the family business."

Before Justus could raise an argument, the butler returned with two men at his side.

"Mr. Erik Lempo and a Mr. Roger Johnston to see you, sir."

Siler turned and greeted the two men, putting his hand on his son's back to indicate his expectation that he stay for the exchange.

"Roger," Siler extended his hand. "How good of you to come. I hope Erik didn't alarm you."

"Well, uh . . . um," the man stuttered, "he didn't exactly give me a choice, so . . ."

"Let's not be dramatic," Erik said slowly. "I simply advised that it would be in your best interest not to dismiss a request from Siler Abbadon." Erik, a tall, thin blond man with striking blue eyes, painted on a manipulative smile.

Roger's Adam's apple bobbed as he swallowed hard. "Yes, of course. Is there a problem, Mr. Abbadon?"

Siler sighed. "Unfortunately, Mr. Johnston, there is. You see, I was reviewing your loan today, and it seems that you're three months behind on your payments. Now, I was remiss in not following up sooner. The first month you were late, I, of course, thought it was just a small error on your part and expected you to pick up where you left off. I then gave you two more months to catch up."

"Oh, that, yes, well, you see . . ." Roger struggled to find the words.

Justus stepped to his left. "I should go. I don't need to be here for this."

"On the contrary, son. If you're going to join the family business, you need to understand *every* aspect of it. That includes having what are sometimes unpleasant conversations with clients." Siler turned his attention back to Roger. "I had Erik bring you here so that we could discuss your options. You see, Roger, I'm willing to work with you. Give you an extension of some kind."

The tension pent up in Roger's body physically left him. His shoulders dropped, and Justus heard his breathing resume to a normal pace.

"Thank you, Mr. Abbadon," he said. "Yes, an extension would be wonderful. Angie needed a new wheelchair, and we just didn't have the extra money for it. It has to be motorized and—"

Siler raised his palm to Roger. "Say no more. We'll just head to my office and negotiate some new terms. But before we do, my son, Justus, is going to go over a few things with you."

Justus leaned in close to his father's ear. "I really don't want to do this," he whispered.

Siler followed his son's move. "We are Mammon demons, son. Others are called to loftier purposes like revenge, but us . . . Our specialty lies in temptation and entrapment. Now, do your duty as not only a demon but as the son of the leader of your legion."

Justus looked at Roger. The man had already been lulled into a false state of confidence, and now Justus was about to inject steroids into that. He looked at his father and then back at Roger, shaking his head. "I'm sorry about this."

Roger furrowed his brow, but didn't have time to ask questions before Justus stepped toward him. Justus locked his eyes on Roger's and did what was expected of him.

"Roger Johnston, you will go with my father and Erik willingly and without hesitation. You will not be afraid when you enter the Chamber. And you will do everything he tells you to do when you get there, and you will feel no pain. When, and only when, you hear the words . . ." Justus paused, a sinister grin turning up one corner of his mouth. "When, and only when, you hear the words *sweet potato pie* you will become aware of your surroundings. At that time, you will believe that Siler Abbadon has given you an extension on your loan and cut your payments in half. And you will be sure to tell everyone you know that Abbadon Finance is a credible and reputable company."

Justus stepped back from the man he had just compelled.

"Happy?" he said to his father.

Siler ignored his son. "Erik, would you please take Mr. Johnston to my office? I'll be there in just a moment. Go ahead and get things started."

Erik nodded, and Roger thanked Siler profusely as he was escorted away.

"I wish you wouldn't do that," Siler said to his son.

"What?"

"Sweet potato pie? Really, it's just ridiculous." He put his hand on Justus's back, directing him to walk with him.

"If you're going to make me do crap like that . . ."

"I should have chosen your mother more carefully. You're too much like who she was before I met her." Siler waved his hand in the air. "It was the twenties. No one *truly* cared about our cause then. They were all just dabbling in it," he murmured.

Justus followed his father to the back of the house, where his offices were, and through a panel in the wall that slid to the side. Dim lighting glowed from the opening. Siler stepped through and descended the stone steps that led to the Chamber. His son followed hesitantly behind him.

The Chamber was about half the size of the back of the estate and was lined with wooden shelves. Each shelf held rows of boxes. Some were covered thickly with dust, while the hinges of others were still shiny and new. One of those boxes sat on the table next to where a compelled Roger Johnston lay strapped to a table with his arms stretched out to either side. His wrists, ankles, and head were secured to the table with leather straps that buckled. Still, the man smiled brightly.

"Mr. Abbadon," he said, "I really can't thank you enough for working with me on the terms of the loan."

"It's truly my pleasure, Mr. Johnston." Siler smiled at him and removed his shirt. "Is everything ready, Erik?"

"Yes, master."

"Very good. Justus?" Siler looked to his son, who hadn't come in much farther than the entrance to the Chamber. Justus shook his head. "Fine."

Siler drew his attention to the table next to Roger. Next to the box lay a knife that looked as ancient as the history of man. The mother of pearl handle was ornately carved with symbols of their legion, having been handed down since the beginning of the Abbadon legion a thousand years ago.

"Is all that really necessary?" Justus challenged.

"No. But the blood pleases the powers that be of the underworld. The happier they are with my performance here, the longer I get to stay like this." He motioned the length of his body, still in prime physical shape despite having walked the earth for almost two hundred years.

He took the knife from the table and held it at his chest with the blade pointed down. Then he closed his eyes and spoke words that only his legion would ever be able to understand.

"Machai enrick romahl." Siler drew the knife down Roger's chest from his collarbone to his navel, just enough to draw blood. "Chaimara enrick Abbadon trehume. Darmar. Sachar." Then Siler slid his hands from the top of the cut to the bottom, smearing the oozing blood. When his hands were sufficiently covered with the thick liquid, Siler pressed his palms to his face and drew his hands down his chest. "Chaimara enrick Abbadon trehume. Damar. Sachar." He pressed both hands to Roger's chest again. "Damar. Sachar. Damar. Sachar. Damar. Sachar." An orange glow emanated from Roger's chest. Erik opened the box and held it near his body. Siler continued to chant, getting louder with each word. "Damar. Sachar. Damar. Sachar. Damar. Sachar." Finally, the orange glow grew brighter and left Roger's chest, hovering above it for a moment before Erik clapped the box around it, trapping it.

Siler stood upright, his own chest heaving from the ceremony. Justus continued to stand nearby, his stoic face telling his father all he needed to know.

Siler turned to him. "One day, son. One day you will fully embrace who we are. Who *you* are. You can't run from it. No matter what you do, you will always be a demon. You will always be an Abbadon."

CHAPTER 8

*I*vy let the hot water of the shower pour over her weary body. Last night's healing episode wasn't unlike others, but for some reason she was feeling especially worn. She chalked it up to the unexpected excitement of the day and the altitude. She dried off and got mostly dressed, waiting to put her jeans on until her body had cooled down. She brushed her wet hair and then twisted it up in a towel on top of her head, then exited the bathroom, and her heart leapt into her throat. There, rocking gently in the corner, was Madame Luiza.

"*Must* you do that?" she asked the old ghost.

"What? I was just waiting for you, dear." Madame Luiza smiled.

"Well, could you maybe, I don't know, knock or something, so I at least know you're out here? You almost gave me a heart attack."

"At least you could heal yourself before you died," she said.

Ivy thought for a moment while she slid her jeans on. She had never thought of that. Could she heal herself? She remembered being thrown by Weston Blaekthorn. The pain that radiated through her body had dissipated within moments of her getting up. Ivy dismissed that level of her abilities to the back burner. There were other things she had to focus on first.

"Yeah, I'm not sure it works like that."

"How about we give it a try?" Madame Luiza painted on a smile too wide for Ivy's comfort.

"How about no." She pulled her long red hair down and worked it with the towel. When it was as dry as it was going to get, Ivy pulled it back and braided it, letting it rest over her shoulder.

"Isn't that why you're here? To figure out your power?" she asked.

Ivy sat on the side of the bed and let out a heavy sigh. "I guess so. I thought I was running away to some benign place where I could hide away and figure it out. I had no idea I'd end up in a place like this. Everywhere I turn, there's some kind of new supernatural person—they're people, right?—next to me. How am I supposed to figure myself out *and* understand this place?"

Madame Luiza stood and met Ivy by the bed. She placed her arm around Ivy's shoulder and somehow pulled her closer.

"Maybe what you need is to stop trying to figure everything out," she said. "Why don't you try just *being*?"

A knock came at the door. Ivy answered it and found Aurelia on the other side.

"That guy is here to see you," she said. The words had barely left her lips before she was walking away.

"Thanks."

Aurelia walked away, and Ivy closed the door. She pressed her lips together in a failed attempt to keep the smile that wanted to burst onto her face from forming. He had said he wanted to see her two days ago, but never showed up, and there was no message indicating he had tried calling the inn.

Ivy turned around and eyed Madame Luiza.

"Be careful, girl," Madame Luiza said. "There are people in this town you should avoid. You already have much to figure out. You don't need that boy clouding your judgment."

Ivy listened to what Madame Luiza said, and gave it its due consideration while she slid on her shoes and grabbed a sweater. But she decided to let her new ghostly friend's first piece of advice take precedence: *follow your gut.*

"Thanks, Madame Luiza," Ivy said with a smile. "I appreciate it but . . . I gotta go."

Madame Luiza gave her a *suit yourself* look and vanished through the wall.

When Ivy landed at the bottom of the stairs, Justus was nowhere to be seen. She poked her head into the parlor and then began down the hall to where the restaurant was when Michaela stopped her.

"He's on the porch," she told her.

"Oh, thanks," Ivy replied.

"Hey," Michaela said, stopping Ivy in her tracks. "I know it's not really any of my business, but you're new here and, well, I was once, too. Sort of. I know what it's like, anyway." Michaela hesitated, seeming to consider her choice of words. "Justus has a complicated life, and I know people will tell you to steer clear of him."

Ivy laughed. "Yeah. Your aunt literally just told me to do that."

"I can see where they're coming from. I know his father's history. But, I know firsthand that reputations aren't always fairly earned. Just because you have a family name doesn't mean you're destined to walk in their footsteps. I also happen to know that those with the worst reputations need friendship—and love—too. It's the perfect antidote." Michaela smiled softly. "I guess what I'm trying to say is . . . don't let what anyone else says about him influence you. Go with your instinct and decide what *you* want. It's your life, Ivy."

Ivy smiled. "Thanks, Michaela."

Michaela retreated to her office, leaving Ivy alone with her conflicting feelings. She was supposed to be concentrating on coming to terms with her ability to heal, not letting her heart skip a beat at the mere mention of Justus.

But, she thought, *I wanted a new life, one where I decided what I wanted. Maybe Cecelia and Michaela are on to something.* Ivy filled her lungs with air and shot it out like a canon. *I won't know unless I try.* She slid on her cardigan and found Justus leaning against the porch railing with his hands in his pockets, one ankle crossed over the other. He bolted upright when he saw her.

"Hey!" His smile was brighter than one would think a demon capable of.

"Hey!" Ivy smiled back.

It was a beautiful day, much cooler than summer days she had experienced in other parts of the country. A breeze whipped through the porch, pulling loose strands of hair from Ivy's braid and across her face. She closed her eyes and reached her hand up to move them. Except, her fingers didn't meet her face. It met Justus's hand. She opened her eyes and found his.

"Sorry," he whispered. "I was just trying to help."

Ivy's heart raced. "It's okay. Really. Thank you." She tucked the loose locks behind her ear and looked at her shoes. "I thought you were going to come by the other day."

"Yeah . . . about that," he stumbled over his words. "I'm sorry. I had some stuff going on with my dad. I wanted to. I *really* wanted to, but . . ."

"It's okay, Justus," Ivy said. "It's not a big deal."

Justus bored serious eyes into hers. "It is a big deal. You've been through enough with not being able to trust people. I want you to trust me."

Ivy stared back at him. She thought about what Cecelia and Michaela had both said to her about Justus. She didn't know if he had mysteriously summoned her to Havenwood Falls, if someone else had, or if it was all a coincidence. But the butterflies taking residence in Ivy's belly were a sure sign that something was going on. And if Ivy was going to buy into an entire town of supernatural beings living under the radar with humans, well then, she could trust the person who saved her from being mauled to death by a shape-shifting werewolf.

"Believe it or not, Justus, I do trust you." The corners of Ivy's mouth turned up just enough to show Justus how she was feeling, but not enough to reveal the depth of that feeling.

"I want to take you somewhere today," Justus declared. "I mean . . . " He sighed. "*May* I take you somewhere today?"

Ivy did her best to stifle the smile that wanted to burst onto her face. "Yeah."

"Great!"

Justus led Ivy to his car, a Tesla Model X, and opened her door for her. Then he drove her away from the town square. Ivy recognized the area as being close to the farmers' market and to the cemetery where she had met Justus. They traveled out of town and on a road called Alverson. The drive was beautiful. Ivy had slept most of the way on both of the buses that had brought her into this valley, so this was the first time she was truly taking it all in. The mountains, several high enough to still have a bit of a snowcap, surrounded them above the trees of the forest that lined the road.

"You okay?" Justus asked. Ivy had been silently staring out the window.

"Yeah, I'm good," she answered. "It's just so pretty."

Justus glanced out the window at the trees and mountains for a moment before focusing his eyes back on the winding road. "It is, isn't it?"

"This can't be news to you."

"It's not." He laughed. "It's just been a while since I've paid attention to it. You've probably seen a lot of beautiful parts of the country."

"Not really. No windows in the back of the RV." Ivy's eyes and voice lowered. "Couldn't have anyone peeking in, seeing the man behind the curtain."

"Hey." Justus reached over and took Ivy's hand. "It's okay. That's not your life anymore." They both looked at Justus's hand clutching Ivy's. She wondered if his heart had stopped as abruptly as hers had. Justus pulled his hand away and gripped the steering wheel.

"So," Ivy said, breaking the silence. "Where are you taking me?"

"I figured if you were going to be in Havenwood Falls, you needed to see *the* falls."

Ivy's eyes lit up. "Really?"

Justus nodded.

"Thank you."

"Don't thank me yet." He smirked.

Ivy ignored his smirk and absorbed the beauty around her. She inhaled deeply, enjoying her existence away from the lies, deceit, and manipulation of her parents. She had only been in Havenwood Falls a few days, but she already wondered if maybe it wouldn't be a layover on her journey, but a new home. Of course, that would all depend on whether she could get a handle on her powers.

Justus parked the car near Cooley Creek and led Ivy down a path to a viewing area near the falls. The wind picked up as they neared the falls, sending a shiver over Ivy's skin. She hugged her body and rubbed her arms to send the goose bumps away. The roar of the falls grew louder until they were as close as they could get and the falls were in full view.

Ivy's jaw dropped as she watched the water roar over the side of the mountain and into the pool before them.

"Now you can thank me."

"It's so beautiful," Ivy said. Then she laughed. "Sorry I sound like a broken record."

"Don't be sorry." Justus smiled softly. "I've been here plenty of times to get away and think, but . . . I've never brought anyone here. It's kind of amazing watching someone see the falls for the first time."

Ivy felt her cheeks flush with heat. But it didn't take long for the mist rising from the falls to begin dampening their skin, causing Ivy to begin to shiver again. Justus removed his hoodie and placed it around Ivy's shoulders.

"I'm so sorry," he said. "I should have thought about how chilly it was over here and how that would affect you."

Ivy pushed her arms through the sleeves and crossed the front over her as she rubbed her arms again.

"It's fine. Thank you for this, but won't you get cold?"

"Um . . . I'm hot-natured." His answer came hesitantly. Ivy studied him for a moment before getting his meaning. He put his hand on the small of her back and escorted her down the path toward Cooley Creek. They walked for a few silent minutes until they found a bench and sat.

"So," Justus began, "healed anyone lately?"

Ivy chuckled. "Nope! I'm trying to stay under the Court's radar." Her laughter turned to sorrow. "But, outside of running in the opposite direction, I don't know what to do the next time. And what if it's a supernatural? The Blaekthorns made it very clear they weren't interested in what I had to offer. More than that, Weston said that his injuries burned like they were on fire. More than *that*, it's against the rules of the Court."

"I'm sure Weston was just being a baby about it," Justus said.

"Addie said I should keep it under wraps, too. I just don't understand why we wouldn't want to help each other with our abilities. I'm trying, but I'm not sure how successful I'm going to be at holding back."

Justus stood and began to pace. His face became pained, and Ivy wondered if she had said something wrong. Was she too new to their supernatural world to consider herself one of them? There were so many rules, it made her head spin to think of it.

Justus ultimately sat back down. He sighed and twisted his hands together. He looked down, wrinkling his forehead as he thought. When he finally looked at her, Ivy saw something in his eyes she hadn't yet seen.

"Then maybe . . . ," he began. "Maybe you shouldn't stay in Havenwood Falls. Maybe you should leave."

CHAPTER 9

*J*ustus's words gutted Ivy. She didn't know what she was expecting him to say, but suggesting she leave town wasn't it.

"I'm sorry." Ivy felt tears of embarrassment begin to form. She stood and took off Justus's hoodie and handed it to him. "Here you are just trying to be nice to me, and I'm sitting here whining. I was supposed to be starting over. Being strong on my own, and all I've been is . . . needy. I'm sorry I spoiled our day." Ivy circled behind the bench with the intention of walking back to town. Justus grabbed her arm before she could go any farther.

"Wait. Where are you going?" Justus stood and met Ivy behind the bench.

"You suggested I leave town, Justus."

"I didn't mean this very second."

"What did you mean?" Ivy tilted her head up to look at Justus, who was now standing close enough to feel the heat emanating from his body.

He ran his hands down his face and almost growled.

"I meant that you should leave town, not because I don't want you here, but because . . ." Justus shook his head.

"Because?" Ivy watched Justus battle with himself. "Justus, if I've said or done something, or if I've seemed to have some kind of expectation of you, I'm really sorry. I don't expect you to babysit me or be my eternal tour guide."

Justus furrowed his brow. "You haven't done anything and . . . I like being your tour guide." He stepped away and rested his hands on his hips. "I, on the other hand, have been a jerk. Worse than a jerk."

"No, you haven't. You saved me from the Blaekthorns' wrath. Made sure I got registered with the Court. Practically carried me back to the inn when I was too weak to walk on my own. And," Ivy smiled, "you introduced me to the best blueberry scone on the planet."

"How is it that you know what I am, but don't care?"

Ivy thought for a moment. "What you were born into doesn't define who you are. Justus, my parents were as human as they came and were the definition of evil. I'm choosing to live a better life than them. I can see that you're doing that, too."

"I don't want you to leave town."

"I don't want to leave."

"Good."

Justus stepped closer and aimed his gaze into Ivy's. She opened her eyes wider in hopes of giving him greater entry into her soul. The electric connection, something Ivy had never felt before, left her breathless.

"I'm going to kiss you now, Ivy."

"Okay." The whispered word had barely left her lips before Justus's were on them. Ivy had a fleeting thought, wondering if something would happen when a demon kissed an angel-fae-human hybrid. She dismissed the thought and settled into the moment, feeling Justus's hands snaking around her waist, drawing her closer to him. Ivy's hands slid up Justus's arms and landed at the nape of his neck. He was soft and gentle with Ivy, and she wondered if somehow he knew this was her first kiss.

Justus pulled away. He tucked a loose lock of hair behind Ivy's ear and smiled as he let his fingers trail across her cheek.

"Um . . ." Ivy bit her lip, unsure of what to say or do.

"I'm sorry." Justus stepped back. "That was . . ."

"Totally okay," she said, finishing the sentence the way she wanted it to end.

"I was going to say *too fast*," Justus continued.

"Yeah." The word spilled out of Ivy slowly. She agreed, but still had no regret.

Justus let out a heavy sigh. "So maybe we pause and slowly ease our way back to the next kiss?"

Ivy pressed her lips together and nodded. The butterflies were back at the mention of kissing Justus again. They sat on the bench and faced each other, letting their knees touch.

"So . . . ," he said.

"So . . . I guess . . . tell me about Havenwood Falls. I have a basic understanding of the rules, but I don't know anything about how it came to be like this. I mean, how does one town become filled with people like you, uh, like us?"

"The town is actually about fifty-fifty between humans and supernaturals, or supes. I've been here a long time, and I still don't completely understand it, but there's something mysterious about this place. The town was settled in 1854, and the founding mages put a spell on the town and part of the area surrounding it so no one can just stumble into Havenwood Falls without them knowing. Many are almost summoned here, in a way. You know, for crowd control."

"I remember being on the shuttle thinking that there was no way anyone would find their way to this place without it. How did all the humans, non-supes, get here?"

"Mayor Stuart's family were founding members. They're human. So were others who came with the founding families. And when they discovered silver and gold in the area, they brought in human miners."

"Oh. That makes sense. So, how long have you been here?" Justus looked out to the water, obviously avoiding Ivy's question. "What's wrong?"

"I don't want to tell you that," he finally said.

"Why not?" Ivy knit her brow together.

"Because it's going to weird you out."

"I'm staying at an inn run by vampires in a town filled with supernatural beings. You're a demon. And I have the ability to heal people. How could whatever you have to say weird me out?"

Justus twisted his body to fully face Cooley Creek. He rubbed his palms over his jeans and stood nervously. He paced in front of Ivy four times before sitting back down and facing her.

"You have to promise me you're not going to freak out."

"I promise. Now, just tell me."

He took a deep breath and settled his gaze on Ivy's face.

"My father and mother met in 1929."

"Did you say *twenty*-nine?"

"Yeah. Twenty-nine. Which is also the year I was conceived."

Ivy blinked what felt like a hundred times. "Um . . . what?"

"I was born in 1930."

"You're . . ." Ivy did the quick math in her head. "Eighty-eight years old."

"Yes."

It was Ivy's turn to twist and face the water. She promised she wouldn't freak out, but if screaming was only in her head, it didn't count as actually freaking out.

Her posture stiffened, and she clasped her hands together on her lap as she tried to comprehend what Justus had explained. Six months ago she would have called him crazy and turned on her heels. Today, though . . .

The freaking out in her head had just about calmed when Ivy flashed back to five minutes ago. She swallowed hard and reached her fingers to her lips.

"That's why I didn't want to tell you," Justus said.

Ivy turned and studied Justus's face. He certainly didn't look like he was eighty-eight. His skin was young, and his hair was full and thick. And his body was, well . . . his body was strong. He looked every bit like an eighteen-year-old guy.

She cleared her throat. "So, uh . . . how does that work?"

Justus rubbed his chin. "It's just the way it is. We don't age the same way as humans do."

"So, what, when you were ten, you looked like you were two?" Ivy questioned.

"Yeah, it was awkward for a while."

"It's awkward now." Ivy thought about this. "So will you keep aging, not aging, like this forever?"

"No," he answered. "At some point we stop aging. So we look anywhere from 50 to 60 years old forever, which is kind of nice. That's also when we're considered accountable to the underworld and have to abide by their rules. Until then, we only have to answer directly to the leader of our legion."

Ivy nodded and let out a heavy sigh. "Okay then."

"Okay?"

"I could try to fight these new realities, but what would that do? You're a demon who barely ages, and I'm an angel-fae-human hybrid with the power to heal people. The fact that you're technically eighty-eight years old isn't the weirdest thing going on in my life right now. I'm not saying it isn't weird at all. I'm just saying . . . I mean, it is what it is, right?"

"Right." Justus smiled and stood. He held out his hand, and Ivy took it as she stood. Disappointment filled her when Justus didn't thread his fingers through hers, instead letting it go. She followed him a few steps before speaking.

"Where to now?" she asked.

"I thought I'd take you up to the top of the falls, then maybe get something to eat at the Fallview Tavern," he told her.

"I need to be back at the inn by four to get ready. Michaela hired me to play in the restaurant a few nights a week. It'll mainly be on the weekend, but she thought a couple of dress rehearsals during the week would be good."

"That's great! I'm glad it worked out. I'll get you back in time, and then I'll come back for dinner so I can hear you play."

"Oh, um, yeah," Ivy stuttered.

"You don't want me to come?"

"No, I do. It's just . . . I'm nervous. I want to do really well, and well . . . you already kind of make me nervous," she said.

Justus's eyes dropped sadly.

"I meant in a good way."

He smiled, and Ivy's heart picked up its pace.

"Well," he said, taking Ivy's hand in his, "I'll be there for moral support. You're going to do great."

Ivy pressed her lips together. They tingled as she thought about pushing up on her toes and planting a kiss on Justus's mouth. She didn't get to act on her idea, though. The sound of a woman calling for help jolted them out of their moment.

The two turned to see a woman who looked to be in her forties rushing out of the forest. Dressed in hiking apparel, she ran toward Justus and Ivy, continuing to call for help.

"Please!" she shouted. "My husband and I were hiking, and he fell. He hit his head, and he's unconscious!"

They followed the woman on the same path through the forest Justus had taken Ivy on to see the falls. They passed the pool at the falls and wound their way another quarter mile through the forest. Ivy knew they were closing in when her hands began to burn and glow. The wife's humanity was proven when she didn't notice it at all.

When they found the man, he was just as his wife had said. His lifeless body lay in a heap about six feet down a hill off the path.

"What do we do?" Ivy whispered to Justus while the woman called reassuring words down to her husband.

"We help them," he said flatly.

"But . . . the rules . . . the Court."

"If we don't help him, he's going to die. If the Court finds out, I'll tell them I made you do it."

Ivy nodded and surveyed the area, looking for the best way to get down to the man, but found no easy path. She looked to Justus.

"Got any ideas?" she posed.

He looked at Ivy and then looked at the frantic woman.

"I do." Justus turned to the woman and took her by the shoulders. "What's your name?"

"Dawn," she answered.

"And what's your husband's name?"

"Doug."

"Okay, Dawn, I want you to just relax, okay?" Justus's voice was calm and soothing. After Dawn nodded, Justus lowered his chin and pierced his darkening eyes into hers. "Dawn, I'm going to go down and get Doug. Nothing about what is about to happen is going to seem strange or out of the ordinary to you. You will only be filled with peace and absolute gratitude for our help. When anyone asks what happened to your husband, you'll say he stumbled and suffered only some minor scrapes. Do you understand?"

"Yes." Dawn's voice and entire demeanor was now calm and collected.

Justus turned around to find Ivy's wide eyes on him. There was no time for him to explain. Justus leapt from the path down to where Doug's body lay. He hoisted the man over his shoulder and leapt back up to the path.

Ivy's jaw slackened. He hadn't revealed his full strength the other night when he helped her back to the inn. Justus had picked up that grown man like he was a bag of feathers.

She stood there for a moment, her mouth agape in amazement.

"Ivy!" Justus barked. She shook her head and brought herself back to the task at hand.

Ivy knelt down next to the man and examined him. There was no blood, but the place above his left ear had quite a goose egg. She pressed her hands to his chest and closed her eyes. When she opened them, her hands continued to burn with heat and glow an almost blinding white. But, for the first time, nothing was happening. Ivy felt nothing in her own body to indicate that any power was moving out of her. She cast her distressed eyes on Justus.

"I don't understand," she whispered.

Justus knelt next to her. "Maybe he's dead," he proposed.

"If he's dead, then why is this happening?" Ivy lifted her hands from Doug's body and shoved them, palms up, toward Justus. She felt Doug's neck for good measure and found a pulse.

Justus's eyes darted around, as if searching for an answer. He finally set them on Ivy.

"I think I know what's wrong," he began. Ivy looked at him expectantly. "He has no soul."

"What? How is that possible?"

"Because it was used to pay a debt."

CHAPTER 10

*J*ustus wasted no time in picking Doug up and carrying him swiftly to his car. Ivy and Dawn jogged behind him to keep up.

"Shouldn't we call an ambulance?" Dawn called.

"There's no time to wait," Justus said over his shoulder.

Ivy was still in shock at having not been able to heal the man. She had no idea there would be limitations to her abilities, not that she understood anything about them. Ivy got in the car as Justus slid Doug into the back seat. Dawn stroked his head gently as she told him to hang on and that he was going to be okay.

All Ivy could do was stare at her hands. She had healed countless people since she came into her powers. Never had it not worked. She tried to make sense of Justus's explanation. How could anyone walk around without a soul? How would Justus know that was the reason Doug couldn't be healed? And what does having or not having a soul have to do with being able to be healed?

They came to a screeching halt in front of the Havenwood Falls Medical Center. Justus shot out of the car and into the emergency room before darting back and opening the door he had slid Doug through only a few minutes earlier. A nurse and orderly emerged from the sliding glass doors with a gurney and took over, gingerly getting Doug on the bed and rolling him inside as Dawn followed and told them what happened.

When the commotion had settled, Justus stood with his hands on his hips, catching his breath. Ivy remained still in the passenger seat. Justus got in and moved the car to a parking space.

"Hey," he said softly. "You okay?"

Ivy gave a beat before she could answer. "I'm not sure."

"He's going to be okay."

"I know." Ivy continued to stare at her hands.

"Then what is it?"

She turned to Justus. "I don't understand why I couldn't heal him."

"You got your power to heal from an angel or a faerie. Souls are a big deal to angels. Makes sense to me that an intact soul would be part of their terms," he said.

"Would have been nice if they had explained that," she replied.

"Everyone has limitations."

"Do you?" Ivy caught Justus's eyes.

"Yes, of course," he answered. Ivy raised her brows to tell him to continue. Justus steadied his steely eyes on Ivy's. "Demons are incapable of love. Nothing they do is out of goodwill. There are always strings attached. Especially my particular *family* of demons."

"Oh."

"It's something I struggle with every day. Something my father wishes I'd just give into so I can go into the *family business*."

"What's the family business?"

He let out a disgusted chuckle. "The family business is the reason you couldn't heal Doug." Ivy's quizzical expression prompted Justus to explain. "My father's company provides personal loans. Most supes don't bother with him because they know what the fine print on the contract is. Humans, on the other hand . . ."

"What's the fine print?" Ivy asked.

"If you default on your loan, Abbadon Finance can collect payment in whatever form the company deems appropriate. My father collects payment in the form of souls. Souls he needs in order to remain the leader of our legion."

"And the Court allows him to do this?" Ivy may have only been in Havenwood Falls a short time, but the position of the Court was made abundantly clear to her.

"The Court can't do anything about it. People sign a legally binding, legitimate contract."

Ivy recalled Justus and Addie's exchange when she registered with the Court.

"Is that what Addie meant when she said you were 'loophole-abiding citizens'?"

"Yeah." Justus's eyes turned down. "We're Mammon demons. Our entire purpose is to tempt and ensnare. We know our only real power lies in our ability to manipulate and trap people. First through the contract, then through compelling."

"Don't say 'we.'" Ivy took Justus's hand in hers. He grasped it tightly. "You may technically be a demon, but you're not one of them," she said. "You said demons are incapable of love, and that everything they do has strings attached. You've had nothing to gain by being so wonderful to me. Nothing to gain by helping Dawn and Doug today. You've acted more like a kind human than anything."

Justus smiled softly and released a breathy laugh. "Maybe my father was right."

"About what?"

"He said he should have chosen my mother more carefully. That I was too much like her."

"Was your mother a human?"

"Yes."

"That's . . . wow. How does *that* happen? Did she know he was . . . you know?" Suddenly Ivy felt awkward. Asking about how Justus came to be seemed to cross an imaginary line. But she had already crossed it, and there was no going back.

"She was a schoolteacher here in Havenwood Falls. From what I understand, rumors of the magic in the falls began to circulate—as they do every once in a while—leading some people to start exploring the dark arts. When my father met her, he thought she was more serious about it than she was. He was in need of an heir, so he compelled her into marrying him. Nine months later, I was born. Just after my third birthday, she was dead."

"I'm so sorry."

"I visit her sometimes," he said.

"Is that why you were headed to the cemetery when we met?" Ivy asked.

"No. That was because I saw you." He smiled. "Her body is at the cemetery, but that's not where I visit her."

"If her body is at the cemetery, she's obviously not cremated. So, where do you visit her?"

"In our cellar . . . where her soul is. Where all the souls are."

Justus Abbadon was becoming more complicated every time he opened his mouth.

Ivy was speechless, and her need for fresh air skyrocketed. She let go of Justus's hand and got out of the car. She didn't want to leave—she just wanted to breathe. It was a good two minutes before Justus got out and met her where she was leaning on the back of the car.

Ivy breathed deeply and rubbed her face with both hands.

"Okay," she began. "Let me just get this straight. Your father's company offers personal loans to people, and when they default on the loan, he takes their soul, which he can do without consequences from the Court because his clients sign a legally binding contract."

"Yes." Justus crossed his arms protectively across his body.

"And he keeps said souls because . . ."

"Because . . . the more souls he keeps in limbo, the longer he gets to walk the earth."

"Limbo?"

"If you die without a soul, you go nowhere. Bodies stay here. Souls go to heaven or hell."

"Nowhere doesn't sound so bad," Ivy offered.

Justus let out a facetious laugh. "No. An eternal waiting room is worse than hell. There is *nothing* there. No joy. No sadness. It's an eternity suspended in a static, catatonic state. Everyone has a right to the eternity they've built for themselves, whatever that looks like."

"What happens if he doesn't collect these souls?" she asked.

"He'll live on earth for a few more hundred years before being cast to the underworld," Justus told her. "He's not crazy about the underworld, so he wants to live topside forever."

"The underworld must be pretty bad if even a demon doesn't want to go there."

"My father enjoys the benefits of the human world too much to give it up. Wealth, women, power."

"What if someone makes good on their loan? He gives them their soul back, right?" Ivy felt she already knew the answer to this, but thought she'd ask anyway.

"I've been tempted many times, but my father . . . He would never do that."

"So why don't you?"

Justus tilted his head curiously. "Why don't I what?"

"Why don't you give Doug back his soul?"

Justus opened his mouth to speak, making a few silent attempts before shoving the words out. "I don't want to think about what would happen if I did that."

"Maybe you should," Ivy said.

Justus stepped away from the car, shuffling his steps as he meandered in front of her. He shook and bobbed his head, seeming to have an argument with himself. Ivy wondered which side was winning.

"The ramifications . . ." he finally said. "I would be disowned. The bond with my father, my legion, would be severed. A demon without a legion is . . . I don't know what that is." Justus's face wrinkled together. The pain he felt even considering such a drastic action was more than it seemed he could bear.

Ivy's heart knew exactly what he was battling. She understood the heartache of realizing that cutting yourself off from the toxicity of your own parents was necessary in order to survive. And knowing that it's for the best didn't make it any easier.

"No one understands what you're feeling right now more than me," Ivy said. Her voice was soft and tender. "It took me six months to do what I needed to do. I pretended I was waiting to turn eighteen, but it was really because I was scared. My parents, my life with them, was all I ever knew. I wanted things to be different, but that was never going to happen. So I had to decide if I wanted to live the rest of my life like that, or if I wanted to be brave and try to make it on my own." Ivy let herself be brave in that moment and took Justus's hand in hers, threading their fingers together. "From the moment I met you, I've watched you behave as anything but how you've described demons to be. If you do this, I believe with everything I am that you're going to be okay. You'll be better than okay."

"One day, I hope I get a chance to thank whoever lured you to Havenwood Falls." Justus wrapped his arms around Ivy and held her tightly. His arms were strong and warm, and any thoughts Ivy had about just passing through Havenwood Falls melted away.

CHAPTER 11

*J*ustus finally released Ivy. He trailed his thumb across her cheek, and Ivy hoped his next move would be to take her face in his hands and kiss her. Instead, he stepped back and shoved his hands in his pockets.

"We should go check on Doug," he said.

"You're right. I haven't noticed anyone else arrive, so Dawn is sitting in there alone."

The two moved toward the entrance to the emergency room. As soon as they passed through the first set of sliding glass doors, Ivy's hands began to heat up. She turned and darted back out into the parking lot, holding her palms out in front of her.

"I can't go in there, Justus," she said. He examined her hands, which had cooled from the distance she put between herself and the infirm. "I don't know what healing that many people would do to my body."

"So don't heal them," he said flatly.

Ivy looked at him like he was crazy. "What?"

"Don't heal them. What would happen if you didn't?"

"I don't know. It never occurred to me," she said. "I've always figured that I was given this gift for a reason. To not use it to help people seems . . . wrong."

"I know you want to help, but you can't heal everyone," Justus said, stepping closer. "The woman at the gazebo, or even Doug in the forest, those are one thing. You could heal everyone in that building, but some of the people in there . . . it's their time to go. You've already seen it happen."

"But what if all they need is one more day? One more moment to make amends with someone? One more opportunity to tell someone they love them?"

"What if one more day lets them hurt another person? Gives them one more day to evade the consequences of their actions. You have no idea. Humans weren't meant to live forever."

Ivy sighed. "So I shouldn't heal anyone, ever?"

"I'm not saying that. I'm just saying that you have to use discretion. Yes, you were given these powers for a reason. But you won't know what that reason is until you try to control it." He dropped his voice so only Ivy could hear. "Besides, some of the docs here are supernatural healers, too. Let them do their job while you learn control."

Ivy eyed the door and then examined her hands.

"I'm scared."

Justus held out his hand for Ivy. She set her trembling hand inside his.

"I've got you."

They had taken only four steps toward the door when Ivy stopped them again.

"Wait," she snapped as she looked at their clasped hands. "They don't just glow. They burn, too."

One corner of Justus's mouth lifted in a small smile. "I can handle heat. I won't let go, Ivy."

Ivy nodded, and they continued into the waiting area of the emergency room.

The heat in her hands rose to its hottest level faster than she'd ever experienced it. Whatever it was in her body that sensed when someone injured or infirm was nearby, it was firing on all circuits, even more than on the busiest night of healing services with her parents. Between the half-dozen people in the waiting room and however many patients already in the building, Ivy wasn't sure how strong she could be.

"You've got this," Justus whispered as he squeezed her hand.

"Your hand is okay?" she worried.

"I told you, I can handle the heat." He gave her a reassuring smile, and they continued through the waiting area to where Dawn was sitting. Her knee bounced anxiously, and she had just about bitten her pinky nail down to a nub. She stood when they reached her.

"I'm so glad you're still here!" Dawn threw her arms around Justus. He wrapped his free arm around her, keeping his word to not let go of Ivy's hand. "Thank you so much! If you hadn't gotten us here as fast as you did, I don't think even Dr. Lewis could have helped Doug."

"We're just glad we were in the right place at the right time," Justus said. "And I have every confidence that Dr. Lewis is going to have Doug out of here in no time."

"Thank you!" Dawn wrapped her arms around Ivy. She didn't want to for fear of what might happen, but Ivy reciprocated and slid her arm around Dawn's waist. Ivy darted wide eyes to Justus. Dawn must have had a small injury of some kind because Ivy felt power leaving her. Justus gently pulled her away and to his side.

"Don't thank me," Ivy said. "I wasn't any help at all."

Justus squeezed her hand in reprimand.

"Don't be silly. You were both a great help."

"Have you heard from anyone how he's doing?" Ivy asked.

Dawn looked over Ivy's shoulder. "Not yet, but Dr. Lewis is coming now."

Justus and Ivy turned to see Dr. Jared Lewis, a handsome African American man walking toward them with a confident, sophisticated gait. He gave them a shadow of a smile as he approached.

"Mrs. Elliott," he began, "Doug is stable. He has some swelling on one part of his brain. We're watching it, but are confident in his recovery. The injury isn't as traumatic as it could have been for someone who hit his head as hard as he did. He's not awake, but you can see him now if you'd like. He's in triage four, but we'll be moving him upstairs soon."

Dawn let out a rush of air. "Thank you, Dr. Lewis." She gave Justus and Ivy appreciative smiles. "Thank you, again."

They nodded and smiled back as she passed them.

"Why in the world would someone be thanking an Abbadon? Then again, compulsion goes a long way, doesn't it?" Contempt dripped from Dr. Lewis's lips.

That was it. The straw that broke Ivy's restraint.

"I don't know who you are, but you have no idea what you're talking about. If it weren't for Justus, that man would be dead."

"Ivy . . . it's okay," Justus said sheepishly.

"No, it's not. Just because your father is who he is, and does the things he does, doesn't mean you should be guilty by association." Heat scorched through Ivy's entire body now. Her eyes penetrated into Dr. Lewis's. She thought she would find anger or disdain, but instead she found sadness.

"Did you really help bring him in?" Dr. Lewis asked. He cocked his head to the side in disbelief.

"Yeah, I did," Justus answered.

Dr. Lewis considered him for a moment and then extended his hand.

"Thank you." The men shook hands, and Dr. Lewis left Ivy and Justus in the waiting room.

"Are you okay?" Ivy asked Justus.

"I'm fine. I'm more concerned about you. How are you doing?" He lifted their still-clasped hands between them.

"It's not getting any worse," she offered.

"Let's just sit. See what happens the longer you're here."

Ivy nodded, and the two sat. She wrapped her free hand around theirs, and Justus closed his around the massive fist. To anyone in the emergency room waiting area, they looked like two people worried about a patient, not a demon and a supernatural hybrid trying to control her powers.

"What did you do to Dawn?" Ivy asked.

"What?"

"I'm trying to distract myself with conversation."

"Well," he began, "you asked if I had any ideas, and the only one I had was to compel Dawn into not seeing what we were going to do."

"Compulsion. What is that, some kind of mind control?"

"Yes."

"Have you done that to me?" Ivy considered how well she thought of Justus and wondered if he had compelled her into it.

"No. Everything between us has been real. And I don't think you should be distracting yourself. You should be concentrating." Justus shot her a look.

"Okay. Fine."

The heat continued to pulsate in Ivy's hands, and the glow streamed out between their fingers like sunlight through clouds. She had never done it before, but she closed her eyes and focused all of her energy on her hands. She thought about the night she wished she could really heal Carla's cancer. Her ability was attached to that wish, so Ivy focused on that moment.

Why did I wish I could heal Carla? Why not anyone before? There had been hundreds of deserving people to come through the line at the healing services. What was it about that night that led to this gift? Ivy's mind raced.

You can't heal everyone. Justus's words rang through Ivy's head.

Ivy continued to concentrate on her hands. Suddenly, they began to cool, diminishing the brightness of their glow. She opened her eyes and pulled her hands from Justus's grasp. They were still warm, and an ambient glow remained, but the intensity that usually coursed through Ivy's body was gone.

"What did you do?" Justus asked.

"I don't know," she answered. "I asked myself why I wished I could heal Carla that night."

"Any answer?"

Ivy considered Justus's question. "That night when Carla came through and my dad sent her away because she didn't pay . . . that was really hard for me. I was the one who refused her money. It was my fault she went home hopeless. I think . . . I think I just wanted to make it up to her. And all those months after, the months I spent healing people, I felt like I was somehow redeeming my family. I mean, we were still charging people, but at least now they were actually getting healed. I think, in some weird way, I've felt like I was paying back a debt. Like I was given this gift to make restitution for how we had lied and deceived and given so much false hope to people in the name of God."

"Don't say 'we.'" Justus looked over his nose at Ivy, echoing her words to him. A sweet grin appeared on his face. "You may technically be their daughter, but you're not one of them. You were a kid, and your options were limited. When you had the chance, you did the right thing, and that's what matters most."

Justus took Ivy's hand and stood. He led her outside and back to the car.

"So," Ivy said, "are you going to take your own advice and do the right thing now that you have a chance?"

"Running away from your parents and breaking the bond between me and my legion are two different things." Justus started the car and pulled out of the parking lot.

"Yours might be more supernatural than mine, but breaking the bond between you and your parents is monumental in both worlds. I'm not saying it'll be easy, Justus. I'm saying that if you want to be free, that's what you're going to have to do."

CHAPTER 12

*J*ustus dropped Ivy off at Whisper Falls Inn in time for her to prepare for her dinner show and made a quick stop at Fairy Tale Florists before heading home. There was a smile on his face that could only come from having spent the day with Ivy. Although it was possible it could have been from Dr. Jared Lewis thanking him for his help. Being a demon was a curse in and of itself. Being an Abbadon in Havenwood Falls only added insult to injury. For a resident to acknowledge Justus's good deed was epic and just might have been the turning point for him to do the hardest thing he'd ever had to do.

He walked through the door and was immediately greeted by the butler.

"Good afternoon, sir. May I take your jacket?"

Justus rolled his eyes. "No."

The man nodded and retreated down one of many dark corridors.

Justus started up the stairs to his room, but paused halfway up. He turned and called to the butler, who met him at the bottom of the stairs within seconds.

"How can I be of assistance, sir?"

"Is my father home?" Justus asked.

"No, sir. He left about an hour ago and said he would be gone for the evening."

"Thank you. That's all."

Justus was left in the foyer, hands on his hips, chin to his chest. He looked to the hall on his left and the door at the end that led to the Chamber. He took long strides and reached the door, stepping through and down the dimly lit stairwell. The lights flickered on, and Justus faced a sight he knew he would never get used to. Hundreds of boxes with souls trapped inside lined the rows of shelves, organized by decade. His father was meticulous in their order.

He wound his way through the Chamber until he came to the shelf where his mother's soul was trapped. Taking it from its place, he sat on the floor with his back against the wall and held the box on his lap.

"Hi, Mom," he whispered. "I'm back. Same crap, different day."

Justus ran his thumb over the wax sealed over the metal latch. His father was prone to taking extra precautions when none were required. No one knew this was how his father kept all the souls he had taken: like a serial killer keeping trophies. It wasn't necessary for him to keep them this way. He could set them free and the souls would roam the earth, still in limbo, not even able to haunt as ghosts because they were separated from their bodies before the body died. It was cruel and sadistic. Par for Siler Abbadon's course.

"I've met someone," he said to the box. "Her name is Ivy, and you're never going to believe this, but she's part angel." Justus laughed. "She's amazing. She's kind and brave, and all she wants is to help people. She is everything I remember about you." He sighed, a small smile lifting the corners of his mouth. "She also believes in me. Believes I can break my bond with the legion. It will be nearly impossible, and it just might get me killed, but I know now that I have to at least try. I want to be like you. I want to completely give in to my human side." Justus nodded his own approval and stood. "I'm going to make this right."

He slid the box with his mother's soul back in place, then moved to an aisle of shelves where he was certain the box he was looking for would be. When he found what he needed, he left the Chamber and darted to his room. He may have just made the biggest decision in his life, but he still had a date to keep with Ivy. He promised he'd be there to support her, and he wasn't going to let her down.

Justus slid his leather jacket over his navy plaid button up shirt and jogged down the stairs and out to his car. The flowers he'd bought for Ivy's debut were still fresh, sitting in the front seat. He smiled, satisfied with his selection, and made his way to the inn.

Approaching the front door of the inn, Justus filled his lungs to capacity and exhaled slowly. It would be obvious to anyone watching that he was nervous.

The door creaked open, and Justus stepped into the lobby and into Addie Beaumont's line of sight. She was sitting in a chair next to Michaela in the manager's office with the door wide open.

"You," she barked at him. "I want to talk to you."

Justus clenched his jaw and prepared for a tongue-lashing.

"What can I do for you, Addie?"

"I talked to Ivy today," she began, with her arms folded across her chest.

"And?"

She waited a long beat. "And she told me what you did." Justus made a hard line with his lips and nodded. "I didn't know you had it in you."

"I've always had it in me. I've just decided to let it all out."

"I'm glad." Addie extended her hand. Justus shook it and smiled. "And I'll be sure to tell my grandmother and the rest of the Court."

Justus's shoulders relaxed, and his eyes widened. "That's very kind of you, Addie. Thank you."

"No problem. Now, go give her those flowers. She's crazy nervous." Addie smiled and resumed her seat next to Michaela in the office. Michaela leaned back and smiled her own approval at Justus. Addie putting in a good word with her grandmother and the Court was a huge deal, but Michaela, an actual member of the Court, giving him her support was priceless.

He found Ivy in the dining room at the back of the inn. Her guitar

hung across her body, and she was lightly plucking the strings and
humming. A face-splitting smile appeared when she saw Justus
walking toward her with a bouquet of flowers.

"They're gorgeous," she said. "Thank you."

"It's your debut performance, and I wanted it to be special."

"Well, even if I suck and the whole thing goes in the toilet, at least
you're here, and that's already made the night special." Ivy shook her
hands out in front of her. "I'm so nervous."

"You're going to do great," he told her. He indicated to her hands.
"How are they, you know, after today?"

Ivy looked at her palms. "Good, I think. I mean, I haven't been
close to anyone sick or hurt, so . . . I guess I won't really know until
that happens. I just hope I can control it like I did at the hospital."

"It might take some practice, but I know you can do it."

Michaela approached them from behind and tapped Ivy on the
shoulder. "You ready?"

Ivy clenched her jaw and smiled nervously. "As ready as I'll
ever be."

"Great," she replied. "No formalities or introductions here. Just
get playin'!" Michaela smiled and walked to the back of the
restaurant.

"You're going to be amazing." Justus kissed Ivy on the cheek and
took a seat at a table to the side of the restaurant. No sooner had he
been given a menu than his father pulled out the chair next to him and
sat. "What the hell are you doing here?"

"Is that any way for you to speak to your father?" Siler Abbadon
slithered.

"What are you doing here?" Justus reiterated.

"I heard there was going to be live music here tonight, and I
wanted to come see for myself," he said.

"Really." Justus didn't hide his skepticism.

"I thought it would also be a good time for you and me to catch
up. You know, dispense some fatherly advice on girls . . . and what
you're supposed to do with the ones who could cause trouble."

"Why are you acting like she's the only healer in this town?"

"Because she's the only one who doesn't control it." Siler's eyes grew darker. "The others know to keep it to themselves."

"She was trying to *help* the Blaekthorn kid," Justus said in Ivy's defense.

Justus could feel Ivy's stare. He looked at her and nodded, answering the question he could tell she was asking: yes, this was his father. He watched as she blew out a rush of air. Then she stretched her neck side to side and stepped up to the microphone.

"Good evening," she said. "I'm Ivy Rapha, and I'm going to sing a few songs for you tonight. This first one is called 'It's Not Over Yet.'" Ivy smiled at Justus.

As she began singing lyrics about fighting your way out of the dark and into the light, Justus's posture changed. The feeling of defeat his father's presence gave him was replaced with confidence.

"Well, *father*, you don't need to worry about Ivy, because she knows how to control her powers," Justus said sternly. "And now that you've done your due diligence and checked up on me, you can leave. Go report back to the rest of your legion lackeys that your son did his job and evaluated a new *threat* to our existence." Justus picked up his menu, but Siler snatched it from him. Before he could speak, Michaela was behind them with a discreetly stern voice.

"Take it outside, boys," she barked in a whisper.

The men shot dagger-filled looks at each other and shoved back from the table. Siler wound his way through the tables first. Justus gave Ivy a knowing look before making his exit. Father and son met on the sidewalk in front of the inn.

"What is going on with you?" Siler demanded. "Is this some kind of human teenage rebellion?"

"This is me having a mind of my own and not being one of your minions," Justus fired back.

"I should have chos—"

"Yes, I know! You should have chosen my mother more carefully. You know what? I'm glad you didn't. I'm glad I'm more like her than I am you."

Siler caught his son's eyes and held them for a long minute. Then he raised his arm out in front of him, his flattened palm facing Justus. Suddenly, Justus's body began to move close to his father, but his feet were slightly elevated off the ground.

Justus crossed his arms in front of his body in an X and then thrust them down, breaking the hold his father had on him.

"STOP!" he shouted.

Siler stepped back, a look of disbelief on his face.

"You dare defy me?" His tone and volume matched Justus's.

"I am *never* going to be like you. Never."

"You are my *son,* and you *will* carry on the great legacy of our legion."

"Like you, *Dad?* Hiding behind your company and squirreling away souls? No, thank you!"

"I suggest you rethink your words, son."

"Or what? Are you going to compel me? Kill me? Take *my* soul?" Justus took five brave steps to close the gap between him and his father. "Do your worst, because your worst will never be as tragic as the life I'm living right now."

Siler stood silent in the wake of Justus's declaration. It may have been the first time in the history of demons that one defied not only his father, but the leader of his legion.

"Now, if you'll excuse me, there's a girl in there singing her heart out, and I promised to be there for her."

Justus left his father standing in the dusky glow of the evening and resumed his seat in the dining room. Ivy was midway through "I've Got You Under My Skin" when Justus gave her a wink and a smile. She smiled back, and Justus hoped he had calmed her nervous heart. She had gone on when he left, but he couldn't help thinking that her mind had raced when he left with his father.

Before he could pick up his menu to review his options, Michaela was at his shoulder. He turned, worried the public altercation with his father had changed her mind about him.

"You're all right in my book, Justus." She pointed at the menu. "Take your pick. It's on the house."

CHAPTER 13

*I*vy woke with a smile on her face even before she opened her eyes. After her set last night, she and Justus had dinner and spent the evening talking about everything *but* his father. She told him about her life growing up on the road, minus the part about all the scamming her parents did, since that was already well covered. Ivy smiled, recalling being homeschooled by both her parents, which were the only times she ever felt like they were a family. She explained how she never knew her grandparents, because her parents said they hadn't approved of their marriage.

Justus told Ivy more about the lineage of his legion in Havenwood Falls and his own bloodline, including that his mother was from a branch of one of the founding families. "That line of the Stuart family died off with her. No one talks about it, so it's pretty much like it never happened."

He smiled when he talked about going to Havenwood Falls High School rather than the private school, Sun and Moon Academy. He didn't understand it then, but he knew now it was because his human side was so strong.

Ivy opened her eyes and relished the burst of colors from the bouquet Justus had given her last night. Michaela was kind enough to let her borrow a vase. She reached her tired arm up and touched the soft petals with the tips of her fingers.

After she stretched and yawned, Ivy sat up to find Madame Luiza asleep in the rocking chair. She cocked her head and smirked.

"I may not know a lot, but I do know that ghosts don't sleep." Ivy chuckled. "Why are you pretending to sleep?"

Madame Luiza peeked at Ivy through one open eye, and then opened the other.

"I thought maybe it wouldn't be as startling for you if I was asleep when you woke up." She smiled mischievously.

"You know what would be less startling? If you knocked sometime."

Madame Luiza laughed. "Oh, you're adorable, dear!"

Ivy shook her head and got out of bed, then went into the bathroom and closed the door.

"So, my dear, how are things going with the boy?" Madame Luiza called through the door. Ivy was glad she didn't literally poke her head in while she was going to the bathroom.

Ivy flushed and called out to her. "I thought you wanted me to stay away from him."

"Yes, yes, I did say that," Madame Luiza said dismissively. "But I had a little chat with my niece, and she seems to think that the Abbadon boy isn't so bad."

"Well, since you've had a change of heart, I think it's going great." Ivy washed her hands and then put toothpaste on her toothbrush. She started brushing and then opened the door. "He helped me figure out how to control my powers yesterday," she mumbled through her foamy mouth.

Madame Luiza smiled. "Oh, that's wonderful! And now tell me what you did for him!" Her eyes were wide with expectation.

Ivy rinsed and spat into the sink. "What makes you think I did something for him?" She left the bathroom, patting her mouth with a towel.

"Justus Abbadon doesn't have a knockdown, drag-out argument with Siler Abbadon for no reason," she said.

"You saw that?"

"I see everything that happens here, my dear," she answered with a little wink.

"Well," Ivy began. "I may have pushed him in the direction of breaking ties with his legion."

"And how would he do that?" Madame Luiza asked.

"By, uh . . . by returning a soul his father took from someone."

"Oh, my."

Ivy sat on the side of the bed. "I know it's going to be hard for him, but is it really an *oh my*?"

"He didn't tell you? Oh, well, he might not know," she mused aloud.

"Know what?" Ivy wondered if she had meddled too deeply in Abbadon affairs that she knew less than nothing about.

"Well, I know only of it from rumors during my short time on the Court, but . . ." Madame Luiza stood and floated to Ivy, propping herself on the bed next to her. The two faced each other like girls sharing secrets at a slumber party. "When a demon breaks the bond he has with his legion, he becomes human. He loses any power he had and becomes mortal."

"Like a fallen angel?"

"That only happens in movies."

"Oh, well, either way . . . I don't know if that will bother him, actually." Ivy felt relieved. "He's much more aligned with his human side, like his mother."

Madame Luiza stiffened her posture. "He's part human?"

"Yeah. I kind of assumed they all were," Ivy said. "But I guess that doesn't make sense."

"Sometimes, when there are no women in a legion, the men must find human women to keep their lineage going. If Justus is already part human, well . . . I'm not sure what will happen to him."

Ivy bit her lip, worried that she had been too hasty in encouraging Justus's exodus from his legion, but thankful for Madame Luiza's information.

"How does a vampire ghost know all this about demon legions?" Ivy asked.

"I already told you, honey. When you've been around as long as I have, you see a lot, hear a lot, and get to know a lot."

"Well, thank you," Ivy said with a sweet smile. "Now I think I need to talk to Justus."

Madame Luiza left Ivy to shower and get ready. They'd arranged the night before that Ivy would meet Justus at Coffee Haven for coffee and blueberry scones. When she arrived, he was already there with her coffee and scone waiting.

Justus stood when Ivy approached the table. He smiled brightly, and she wondered how resilient the human nature inside him had to be in order to outweigh the demon side. She wanted him to be happy, to be free. But she was scared of what awaited Justus if, or when, he broke the bond with his legion. Would he become fully mortal? Would his chronological age catch up with him? How much more time would they have together?

Her face must have betrayed her, because Justus took her by the shoulders and leaned down to look into her eyes.

"Ivy, are you okay? What's wrong?" he begged.

Ivy blinked a few times and gave her head a small shake. "I'm sorry," she said. "Didn't mean to worry you. I'm fine. Just . . . thinking about, well, you."

He pulled her chair out, and Ivy sat.

"You look sad. Thinking about me makes you unhappy?" he asked, sitting.

"No, not like that. I was thinking about what we discussed. About you giving Doug back his soul."

"Oh, I see. And why did that upset you? I thought you were all for me leaving my legion." Justus took a bite of scone and chased it with a sip of coffee.

"I am. I'm just concerned about what that's going to mean for you. After. When you're no longer connected to your father or your legion. You'll be a demon orphan. Will you still have your strength and your ability to compel? How will you age?" Ivy sighed. "I didn't know if you knew what would happen to you, or if you didn't, if you had considered it. I just want you to be okay."

Justus laid his hand on the table, palm up, inviting Ivy to take it. She rested her hand in his, and he wrapped his fingers around hers.

"That right there is exactly why I'm ready and willing to take this risk," he said. "I'm 88 years old, and everything after my third birthday has been void of that level of kindness. That part of me has always been there, bubbling up, hoping to boil enough to blow the lid off the pot." Justus ran his thumb across Ivy's knuckles. "All I needed was a catalyst. And then you showed up." Ivy tried to stifle her smile, but gave up and gave into it. "I don't know what's going to happen. I just know I have to do this. I'm hopeful it ends well, because I'm just getting to know you, and I don't want to stop."

"I don't want it to stop either."

Justus grinned. "Good. Now, I think I have a plan, but I don't think it will work without some help."

"What kind of help?" Ivy asked.

"The kind of help that isn't usually offered to demons."

Ivy took a long sip of her coffee and turned the cup around in her hands. She set it down and locked her eyes on Justus's. "I know exactly who to ask."

CHAPTER 14

*I*t took four days, but everything was in place. Justus told Ivy he wasn't worried, to which Ivy responded was the biggest lie she had ever heard. The plan, as it developed, became bigger than Justus first imagined. And because it was now the monster that it was, it also had the potential to blow up in all their faces.

Before Justus left home, he did something he had stopped doing years ago: he compelled someone for his own benefit. Ultimately it would be for the benefit of everyone in Havenwood Falls, but the first step was for him. He also reasoned that it was only the butler, who already existed in a compelled state, thanks to his father.

Justus picked Ivy up at the inn, and the two traveled in silence to the Havenwood Falls Medical Center, where Doug Elliott was still a patient. Dr. Lewis had worked his magic, and the swelling on Doug's brain had gone down. He had been conscious since yesterday, and according to Dawn, "already back to his usual annoying self."

The two remained silent in the car for a few moments even after Justus turned the engine off in the parking lot. Ivy looked at him and could practically see the thud of his heavy heartbeat. She took his hand in hers.

"Are you okay?"

He let out a cleansing breath. "I think so." He turned to her. "Are you?"

"I'm fine, but I'm not the one about to bust his father for the loopholes the Court doesn't know about."

"Ivy," he began, "I really don't know what's going to happen when all is said and done. I don't know if my age is going to catch up with me, or if I'll die on the spot."

"Don't say that," she protested.

"The reality is any number of things could happen. And I know I said we were going to slow down, but . . ." He paused and searched Ivy's eyes. "If I don't kiss you again before everything goes down, I'll regret it for the rest of my life, however long or short that may be."

Without another syllable, Justus's hand was behind Ivy's neck, pulling her to him. Their lips crashed together, moving in perfect sync. Ivy took a fistful of Justus's shirt in an effort to pull him closer as his free hand found her thigh. Were their bodies not twisted in the front seat of a car, their kiss had the potential to erupt into something that would definitely *not* constitute taking things slowly.

Justus pulled away and cupped Ivy's face in his hand. His thumb grazed her cheekbone, now harder to find under the pillow of flesh made by Ivy's smile.

"I hope I don't, but if I do, I'll die a happy man today."

Ivy took Justus's face in both hands. "You are *not* going to die today."

"I guess we're about to find out."

Ivy readied herself as the two entered the medical center through the main entrance. Although she hadn't been in since he awoke, Ivy had visited Doug in the days since he had been admitted to give Dawn some company and a break when she needed it, but mostly to practice keeping her power in check. The glowing had reduced to almost nothing, and the heat that once burned in her hands was now a bearable warmth. Ivy felt confident that if she could control her body's response to its need to heal in a hospital, everyday life would be more than manageable.

Justus fixed the strap on his backpack as they entered the elevator.

He gripped Ivy's hand a little more firmly as they made their way to Doug's room. When they arrived, Dr. Lewis was next to Doug's bed, a tray of tools on a rolling table next to him. He checked his watch.

"Right on time," he said.

"Who's this?" Doug asked.

Dawn smiled from ear to ear. "These are the people I told you about," she said. "They saved your life by getting you here in time."

"Oh, wow, yeah . . . thank you so much." Doug extended his hand. Justus immediately reciprocated.

"Mr. Abbadon, Miss Rapha, can I see you in the hall for a moment?" Dr. Lewis asked. They followed him out and down the hall a few paces. "You're sure this is going to work?"

"If everyone does their part, yes," Justus replied.

"Well, then." Dr. Lewis smiled. "Good luck, Justus."

A nurse walked by and addressed Dr. Lewis. "There's that smile we all know and love!"

"A new baby girl will do that to you," he said with a chuckle.

"Congratulations," Ivy said with a smile.

Justus stuck out his hand. "Congratulations."

"Thanks. Now, let's get this show on the road."

Dr. Lewis left Justus and Ivy to tend to his part of the plan, which was minor compared to other cogs in this machine. When the two returned to Doug's room, Ivy sat next to Dawn. She watched how happy the couple was. Had they known that Siler Abbadon had scammed Doug out of his soul, would they each live in this kind of happiness? Ivy smiled, because it didn't matter. Before the hour was up, Doug would have his soul back, and no one in that hospital would know anything happened.

It was Ivy checking her watch this time. Seeing that everything should be in place, she nodded once at Justus. He took a deep breath and put his backpack gently on the chair on the opposite side of the room. Opening it, he took out the box that contained Doug's soul. Then he looked at Dawn as he had that day on the path.

"Dawn, you're not going to hear anything I'm about to tell Doug. In fact, you're feeling very tired and think you should rest your eyes until I tell you to wake up." She nodded, closed her eyes, and dropped her chin to her chest. Justus turned his attention to Doug before he could respond to what he had just seen. "Doug, you heard nothing that I just said to Dawn. You're feeling very tired and want to sleep until I tell you to wake up." Doug also nodded, then he closed his eyes and let his head fall to one side on the pillow.

Justus looked at Ivy. "You sure you want to be here for this?"

"I'm not going anywhere, Justus."

A wave of power suddenly shook the building. Ivy bolted to the nurse's station at the end of the hallway and saw that everyone was frozen, just like Justus said would happen.

"You'd better work fast," she told him when she came back into the room.

Justus pressed his hand against the wax seal over the metal latch and closed his eyes. Ivy watched as the wax melted onto the table. Before Justus could open the box, the clack of expensive loafers echoed their slow steps in the hall. Justus worked quickly. He opened the box and scooped his hand under the orange glow of Doug's soul. It pulsated as it floated above his open palm, like it knew it was about to be returned to its home. Ivy's eyes widened at the sight.

Justus held the soul above its rightful home and took a deep breath.

"Romahl enrick machai. Trehume Elliott enrick chaimara."

Doug's soul glowed brighter and pulsated with excitement. It leaped from Justus's hand and hovered above Doug's chest.

Ivy swallowed hard as the footsteps grew closer.

"Sachar. Damar. Sachar. Damar." Justus began to chant.

As Doug's soul grew even brighter and bounced happily above its owner, Ivy thought their mission was about to be completed. She knew she was mistaken when her body was suddenly thrown across the room and stuck to the wall. The culprit stood in the doorway.

"Manoch!" Siler Abbadon's wicked voice boomed as Justus took his turn sliding across the floor. The man slithered in, examining Justus and Ivy with sinful eyes. Without a word, he moved to Doug's bedside.

He reached out to take the soul that was desperately waiting to be returned, but a spark ignited when he touched it.

"You're too late!" Justus shouted.

Siler turned to him. "It's never too late to take what is rightfully yours."

"You conned him out of his soul just like you did all the others!" Ivy barked.

"A signed contract is not a con, my dear," Siler said as he scanned the room, his eyes landing on the tray of instruments. He inhaled impatiently. "But now I'm going to have to get my hands dirty again in order to reclaim his soul. Pity. This is one of my favorite suites."

He picked up a scalpel and cut down Doug's hospital gown. The scar from his first encounter with the demon was faint, but still there. With Doug's chest clear of obstruction, Siler put the knife to Doug's chest and began to cut.

No sooner had a drop of blood emerged from Doug's body than Ivy's feet were hitting the floor and Justus was standing at her side. Siler's head snapped to one side, shock painting his face at the two having been released from his hold. They didn't charge forward in any effort to stop him. He smiled victoriously and turned back to his victim, continuing to cut. When the knife would move no farther, he looked back at Justus and Ivy, only they were no longer alone. Standing next to them were several members of the Court of the Sun and the Moon.

CHAPTER 15

$\mathcal{S}$iler tossed the scalpel onto the table and squared his shoulders in a defensive stance. He lowered his chin and set his dark eyes on Saundra Beaumont. Mathilde Augustine and Roman Bishop, Saundra's counterparts in the High Council of the Luna Coven, stood shoulder to shoulder with her. Michaela caught Ivy's eye and gave her a knowing wink.

"It's over, Dad," Justus declared.

"You're right," Siler agreed. "It's over, because there's nothing they can do. I have a signed contract from this man and everyone else whose soul I am now in possession of. They know that. Don't you, Saundra?"

Saundra stepped forward.

"Siler Abbadon, you are hereby in violation of the laws of the Court of the Sun and the Moon," she said with official eloquence.

"You're grasping at straws," he barked.

Roman Bishop lifted his hand and twisted it quickly. Siler's arms became ramrod straight at his sides. He tried to move, but with another flick of Roman's wrist, it was Siler's turn to be glued to the wall.

Siler set his eyes on Saundra as a demon would to compel his victim.

Elsmed Fairchild stepped forward. "Don't even think about it," he warned.

"You may have a contract that says you can collect payment in whatever form your company deems appropriate, but the laws of the Court supersede your contracts when you willingly harm a human resident of Havenwood Falls," Saundra continued. All eyes turned to the small pool of blood gathered at the top of Doug's chest. Ivy didn't want to think about how much blood was shed for all the souls Siler had taken. "You had your loophole to collect souls. What you don't have is any defense that will get you out of this."

"I'll have my day in front of the Court," he declared.

"The Court is here now. We have a quorum, who have all witnessed your flagrant violation of our laws. Shall we vote?" Saundra turned to make eye contact with the other members of the Court. "All those who find Siler Abbadon guilty of intentionally harming a human resident of Havenwood Falls, cast your reply by a show of hands." Almost in unison, all hands rose in the air. "Siler Abbadon, you have been found guilty of intentionally harming a human resident. Your legion is hereby banished from Havenwood Falls for all eternity. Your legion will leave with all it arrived with. Anything, including the souls you acquired through deceptive practices, will remain within the city limits of Havenwood Falls."

Siler's eyes turned black. He clenched his jaw as his face became a shade of red Ivy thought most resembled the devil himself. He cast his fiery gaze on his son.

"See what you've done? You've ruined everything we had here. Kiss your girlfriend goodbye, because you're never going to see her again."

"We have our own loopholes, Siler," Saundra said. She looked at Justus and dipped her chin.

Ivy squeezed Justus's hand before he stepped toward Doug, breathing slowly, his heart pounding inside his chest. He looked again at the small pool of blood that sat on Doug's chest.

"Justus," Siler called. "*Son.*"

Justus turned to his father. "Not anymore." He extended his arms and cupped them over Doug's soul. The orange, glowing ball of light moved around almost anxiously. "Sachar. Darmar. Sachar. Darmar." Justus resumed his chant. "Romahl enrick machai. Trehume Elliott enrick chaimara. Sachar. Darmar. Sachar. Darmar."

Doug's soul elevated a good five feet above his body, then rocketed down, penetrating his chest and sending a bolt of energy through it like he had been shocked with a defibrillator.

Ivy let out the breath she had been holding and rushed to Justus's side. They wrapped their arms around each other, both seeming to wait for a proverbial shoe to drop, since they had no idea what might happen to Justus. Ivy took Justus's face in her hands and stared into his eyes. Searching. Waiting. Nothing happened. Nothing until the commotion where Siler stood.

"No!" Siler shouted. "NO!"

Everyone watched as dozens of dark, shadow-like hands reached through the wall and floor, grasping and pulling at Siler. He struggled to break free from their grip, but it was useless. They pawed at his face, covering his eyes and his mouth. They tugged at his arms and legs, until he began to sink into the wall and all that could be heard were his muffled cries.

Then he was gone.

Ivy stepped back from Justus. She examined him from head to toe, waiting, again.

"Is that it?" she asked. "I mean . . . are you free?"

"I think so."

Saundra Beaumont stepped forward and put her hand on Justus's shoulder.

"Well done," she said. "We're all very proud of you." She turned to the other members of the Court. They smiled and nodded and showed their pride in each of their own ways. "Now, to make this official . . ."

"Make what official?" he asked.

Saundra smiled. "Justus Abbadon, you have found favor with the Court of the Sun and the Moon. You exposed Siler Abbadon's deeds, enabling the Court to banish the Abbadon legion from Havenwood Falls.

By breaking your bond with your legion, you have done what no demon has ever done. You have the eternal trust and the protection of the Court."

"If the legion is gone, who would he need protection from?" Ivy's timid voice interrupted.

"Only those who have reached accountability within their legion will be banished," Saundra said.

"So the other sons in the legion . . . they're still here," Justus said.

"Yes, but as I said, you have the full protection of the Court. You have done us a great service, Justus. Thank you." Saundra shook his hand. "And thank you, Ivy. From what I understand from Michaela and Addie, were it not for you, Justus may not have had the courage to expose the dealings of his legion."

"He just needed someone to believe in him."

Justus slid his arm around Ivy's waist and hugged her closer to his side.

"So, you don't have any of your powers," Ivy said as she looked at Doug and Dawn. "Um . . ." How would they be brought out of their compelled state if Justus no longer had the power to compel?

"The Luna Coven has temporarily handled that," Saundra said. "Ivy said you wanted to make things right. We have granted you power to compel until the next full moon." Her eyes darted between Justus and Ivy. "And on the recommendation of my granddaughter, we've ensured your aging won't be an issue."

Justus inhaled deeply. "Thank you."

Saundra turned and addressed the Court. "It looks like we're done here. However, I think a conversation with the Abbadon legion sons who remain in Havenwood Falls would be a good idea. Best to let them know we'll have our eye on them, in case they get any ideas about picking up where Siler and their fathers left off."

The Court shuffled out of the hospital room, leaving Justus and Ivy standing next to Doug's bed.

Ivy let out a heavy sigh. "Do you feel any different?"

"No, actually."

"And you're not going to turn into the Crypt Keeper or anything!"

"I'd definitely call that a win." He smirked. "Because then it'd be super weird to do this." Justus leaned in and kissed Ivy like a man who had just cheated eternal damnation. His hands gripped her waist, pulling her closer. Ivy responded accordingly and slid her hands up his arms to find the nape of his neck. Had they not been interrupted, Ivy was sure she could kiss Justus all day.

"Eh-hem." Dr. Lewis stood in the doorway with his arms folded, a subtle smirk on his face. "I take it everything went as planned."

"Yes," Justus said. "Thanks for your help."

"All I did was leave the necessary surgical tools in here," he said.

"Don't underestimate your help," Justus said. "Without that scalpel nearby, the Court never would have witnessed his violation."

Dr. Lewis smiled and nodded once.

"Is everyone else okay?" Ivy asked.

"The Luna Coven's protection spell on the hospital worked perfectly," Dr. Lewis said. "It went into effect just before Siler arrived, which made him believe he had been the one to freeze time in the building."

"I'm so glad," Ivy said with a sigh of relief.

"These two, though, could use a little help." Dr. Lewis motioned to Dawn and Doug, who were still sound asleep.

Ivy looked at Doug's chest and the small wound that had been made.

"May I?"

Dr. Lewis cocked his head to the side, seemingly considering his answer.

"I got him this far. You can handle the rest."

With her new ability to control her powers, Ivy wondered if healing would have the same effect on her body as it had before. She reached her hands out over Doug's body and pressed them to his chest. Justus and Dr. Lewis watched as the blood dried up and disappeared, the new incision healed, and the faint scar from the first time Siler Abbadon cut into him completely faded away.

"Impressive," Dr. Lewis said. "But stay out of my hospital." He gave Ivy a wink and left the two to rouse Dawn and Doug from their slumber.

"How was that?" Justus asked her.

Ivy searched her body for signs of fatigue that always followed her healing someone and found nothing.

"Amazing! I don't feel anything. I mean, I felt it when it was happening, but there's nothing now." Ivy beamed. "You ready to take care of them?"

Justus agreed and looked at Doug.

"Doug, you're ready to wake up now. You're going to feel better than you ever have before, and you're not going to notice that your hospital gown is torn. Dawn, you're ready to wake up now. You're not going to notice that Doug's hospital gown is torn. It will be as if no time has passed."

Husband and wife opened their eyes and picked up the conversation with Ivy and Justus where they had left off.

"I can't thank you enough for how you helped that day," Doug said. "It could have been way worse than it was."

"It definitely could have been worse," Justus said. "I'm just glad you're okay."

Dr. Lewis appeared at the door with a pleasant smile. "Good news, Mr. Elliott: you're being discharged!"

Justus and Ivy said their goodbyes to Dawn and Doug and exchanged knowing looks with Dr. Lewis as they left the room.

"So what do I do now?" Justus mused as he pulled out of the parking lot.

"I guess you go home," Ivy said, smiling.

"I'm not sure if I even have a home to go to." Justus took Ivy's hand in his. "Will you come with me?"

"Of course."

CHAPTER 16

*T*hey arrived at Justus's house to find Cecelia Amundson sitting on the front steps. Ivy and Justus exchanged puzzled looks before they got out of his car. Cecelia stood as they approached, a sweet smile on her face.

"Cecelia," Justus said by way of greeting.

"Hello, Justus. Ivy."

"Is there something I can help you with?" Justus asked.

"I came here to help you," she told him.

"Oh, well," he began. "Would you like to come in?"

Cecelia nodded, and the three entered the house. It was dark and quiet, and unusually cold. There was no butler there to greet them. No other household servants in his place. With Siler Abbadon sucked into the underworld, the compulsion they were under was broken, sending them back to the lives they had before.

Cecelia stood in front of Justus and Ivy, looking like she could barely contain whatever it was she had come there for.

"Can I get you anything?" Justus offered.

"No, thank you," she answered. "I've come with news for you, Justus."

He furrowed his brow. "News from whom?"

"From the Dominions."

"Am I in trouble?" Justus's eyes turned into saucers.

"Heavens, no!" Cecelia grinned.

Ivy cleared her throat, already confused by Justus and Cecelia's exchange.

"Who are the Dominions?" she asked.

Justus looked at her, his eyes still wide. "They're angels," he told her.

"Yes. They regulate the duties of lower angels," Cecelia added.

"Like a supervisor?"

Cecelia chuckled. "Kind of."

"So what do they want with Justus?"

Cecelia couldn't hide her joy. "They want to thank you," she said to him. "No demon has ever broken the bond with their legion before. You became fully human today, Justus."

"Oh, well . . . tell them I said you're welcome?" Justus didn't seem to know what the correct response should be.

"I'm not done, silly," Cecelia said. "They've been watching you, hoping you would make the choice you did today. Now that you're fully human, the angels can use you to do great things."

"That's wonderful," Ivy said. She took Justus's hand in both of hers.

"I'm here to tell you the first thing they plan on doing." Cecelia inhaled and let out the beam of happiness she had been trying to control. "You will become an angel, Justus."

"What? How is that even possible?" he stuttered.

"Apparently they can do whatever they want!" Ivy laughed. "Look at me!"

"You've been sanctified. You forgave a debt with no benefit to yourself. In fact, you were willing to die in order to do it. So, you will be a Princedom angel because you will guide and protect, just like you did today. You will also carry out tasks given to you by the upper sphere angels and, best of all, give blessings to the world."

"This . . . this . . ." Justus couldn't seem to find the words.

"This is everything you've ever wanted," Ivy said, finishing his sentence. "Thank you, Cecelia."

"Don't thank me," she said. "The angels have a way of getting what they want. I wasn't kidding when I said Justus may be the reason you found yourself in Havenwood Falls." Cecelia moved to the front door and opened it.

"Wait," Justus followed after her.

"I'll need to compel people in order to give their souls back to them," he said. "Is that going to be a problem with the Dominions?"

"Of course not," Cecelia answered. "You wouldn't be compelling for your own selfish gain. The angels consider the condition of your heart, and your heart's desire is to make things right."

Justus sighed. "One more thing. How am I supposed to know what to do? I don't know how to be an angel."

Cecelia put her hand on his shoulder. "Don't worry, Justus. You know more than you think."

Ivy closed the door behind Cecelia and looked up at Justus. Tears streamed down his face, and all he seemed to know to do was wrap his arms around Ivy.

"I'm so happy for you," Ivy whispered into his ear. "All you wanted was your freedom, but you got so much more."

Justus released her and wiped the tears from his face.

"I couldn't have done this without you. And apparently, I know whom to thank for your arrival in Havenwood Falls now." He let out a breathy laugh.

Ivy turned and finally noticed the grandeur of the foyer they were standing in. Three of the RVs she grew up in could easily fit within its walls.

"So . . . are you going to stay here?" she asked.

"Not for long," he answered. "But I can't leave yet."

"Why not?"

"I'll show you."

Justus led Ivy down the steps to the cellar where the Chamber was. It was cold and damp, just as she expected it to be. The lights flickered on, and Ivy gasped at the rows of shelves filled with boxes. After seeing the box Doug's soul was in, she knew immediately what she was looking at.

"So this is them," she said. "All of them?"

"All of them. Honestly, I didn't know if they'd still be here," he said. "What am I supposed to do with them?"

"Isn't it obvious? You're going to return them. As many as you can. You're going to give people their souls back."

Justus put his hands on his hips and walked down the main aisle. "There are so many that can't be returned."

"Maybe the Court can help you with that, too," Ivy suggested.

Ivy met him where he stood. She saw the sadness and desperation in Justus's eyes and understood. There's a moment when you realize the enormity of getting the only thing you've ever wanted. She felt it as soon as the bus pulled away from the station in Gunnison. It's a mixture of celebration and utter terror. Justus had more on him than Ivy did, because of how many wrongs he had to right. But Ivy wasn't worried. If Justus could defeat his father and send him screaming into the underworld, there wasn't anything he couldn't do.

Justus turned to Ivy. "Will you help me?"

"Absolutely."

"It might take a while." He smiled.

Ivy took both of Justus's hands in hers. "That's okay. I'm not going anywhere."

WE HOPE you enjoyed this story in the Havenwood Falls High series of novellas featuring a variety of supernatural creatures. The series is a collaborative effort by multiple authors. Each book is generally a stand-alone, so you can read them in any order, although some authors will be writing sequels to their own stories. Please be aware when you choose your next read.

Other books in the Young Adult Havenwood Falls High series:

Written in the Stars by Kallie Ross
Reawakened by Morgan Wylie
The Fall by Kristen Yard

Somewhere Within by Amy Hale
Awaken the Soul by Michele G. Miller
Bound by Shadows by Cameo Renae
Inamorata by Randi Cooley Wilson
Fata Morgana by E.J. Fechenda
Forever Emeline by Katie M. John
Reclamation by AnnaLisa Grant
Avenoir by Daniele Lanzarotta
Avenge the Heart by Michele G. Miller
Curse the Night by R.K. Ryals (August 2018)
Blood & Iron by Amy Hale (September 2018)

More books releasing on a monthly basis.

Stay up to date at www.HavenwoodFalls.com

Subscribe to our reader group and receive free and exclusive stories and more!

ABOUT THE AUTHOR

AnnaLisa is the youngest of four children and the only daughter, born and raised in Fort Lauderdale, Florida. After graduating high school, she moved to Charlotte, North Carolina, with her parents. This turned out to be a blessing, since it was just a few short years later that she met her husband in the Film Actor's Studio of Charlotte.

AnnaLisa completed her undergraduate degree in Human Services at Wingate University and her master's degree in Counseling from Gordon-Conwell Theological Seminary. During her thirteen years in the Human Services field, AnnaLisa worked with children in group homes and foster care, and spent two years in private practice counseling individuals, families, and couples.

In 2013, after all three YA novels in The Lake Series were written and she had let them sit long enough, AnnaLisa took matters into her own hands and self-published the titles within just a few months of each other. Received well by readers young and not-so-young alike, The Lake Series has enjoyed breakout success, selling close to half a million copies the first year.

AnnaLisa is represented by Italia Gandolfo of GH Literary. She has been married to her super awesome husband Donavan since 2001 and lives in North Carolina with their two ridiculously cool kids.

ACKNOWLEDGMENTS

I'm so grateful to the amazing family of Havenwood Falls authors. There is no way to be part of this community and not feel loved and supported. Thank you to the incredible Kristie Cook for letting me be a part of this magical place. And to Michele G. Miller for convincing me over delicious barbecue that writing Ivy's story would be life changing. You were so right!

Thank you to my agent extraordinaire, Italia, for being the co-captain of my cheerleading squad. Your belief in me and my work means more to me than you may ever know. The best is yet to come!

Thank you to my readers for coming on this incredible journey with me. You have stamped your passports through every genre of my storytelling, encouraging me with every stop. Thank you! Thank you! Thank you!

And to my husband, Donavan, and my amazing kids, Truman and Claire: you are the captains of my cheerleading squad! Thank you for always believing in me. Your love and support for every crazy dream and idea I have is the reason I can fill the pages!

HAVENWOOD FALLS HIGH

Avenoir

DANIELE LANZAROTTA

~ A Havenwood Falls Young Adult Novella ~

Avenoir (A Havenwood Falls High Novella) by Daniele Lanzarotta

Heidi Bennett had the perfect life—including great parents and an insanely romantic boyfriend—until it all came to a screeching halt the night of the Cold Moon Ball last December. Now, months after her disappearance, Heidi walks among the residents of Havenwood Falls once again, but most—whether human or supernatural—can't see her.

The last thing Heidi remembers was dancing with her boyfriend at the ball. Her disappearance, and the events surrounding it, remain a complete mystery. One she's determined to solve.

Zane is a guardian angel with a history of making questionable choices. As punishment for one such decision, he's ordered to stay with Heidi while she fulfills her mission. But he struggles with his choices yet again when he finds himself in the middle of a dangerous game—a game whose outcome could have eternal consequences not only for him, but for Heidi as well. And only one of them can win.

AVENOIR

AN EXCERPT

DECEMBER 2017

I look at my reflection in the mirror, and I think about backing out of the Cold Moon Ball for the hundredth time. Tonight should feel perfect. This is one of my favorite events in Havenwood Falls. My long light-blue dress is absolutely stunning, and Mom insisted that I borrow this beautiful silver crown she won at a pageant, but none of it takes my mind away from this gut feeling that something bad is going to happen.

"You look beautiful," Mom says. I turn around, and she's leaning against the doorframe, keeping her distance, as she has been sick over the past few days.

I bite my bottom lip, feeling uncertain about this whole night.

"What's going on?" she asks.

I take a deep breath and glance down toward the infinity symbol on the promise ring Jace gave me last year for my sixteenth birthday. Without taking my eyes off the ring, I say what has been on my mind since last night, when I talked to him. "Jace said he needs to talk to me about something important."

Mom tilts her head to the side and gives me a reassuring smile. "I hope you don't think he's breaking up with you. You two have been together since middle school, and you get along better than most adult couples I know." She laughs.

I feel myself relax. She's right. I've just never heard him sound so serious before.

The doorbell rings, and Mom smiles again. "I'll get it. I'll let him know you will be down in a bit."

I look at the mirror one more time, take a deep breath, and tell myself to get it together.

As I walk out of my room, I see Jace at the bottom of the stairs, with his back to me. He's wearing black pants and a black peacoat. I can almost guarantee that instead of a dress shirt, he's wearing an old band T-shirt under his coat. The thought of that makes me laugh for a split second, before that gut feeling consumes my every thought yet again. As I make my way down the stairs, I even manage to fake a smile. The moment Jace turns around and looks up at me, his mouth hangs open, and I know by the way that he stares at me that Mom is right. Just like that, the fake smile quickly turns into a huge grin.

We say goodbye to my mom and head outside. Jace puts his hand on the small of my back as we walk away, and I freeze in place when I see his dad's black Camaro convertible parked on the street.

"Do you want to drive?" he asks, and my eyes widen.

I laugh and look at him. "You're kidding, right? I'm surprised your dad let you drive his favorite child."

Jace chuckles, showing off his dimples. He always jokes about his dad loving that car more than anything or anyone else.

"There is no way I'm driving it," I say.

He grins at me. "We should get going. We already missed the first part of the evening."

As we drive up toward Havenwood Heights, Jace turns the music up loud, and I find myself distracted by the Christmas decorations along the way. When I was little, Dad used to bring me to this area every Christmas and just drive around. And no matter how many times we did that over the years, the sight of the large houses with

Christmas lights glowing, and Mt. Alexa in the background, is always breathtaking.

When we get to the Mills mansion, one of the biggest houses on the street, Jace parks his dad's car as far away as possible from other cars around.

"Wait." He stops me when I reach for the door. He gives me a crooked smile before he gets out and rushes to my side. He opens my door and extends his hand to me. Once out of the car, I see just how far we have to walk. I laugh. "You did have his permission to take the car, right?" I ask jokingly.

Jace chuckles as he slips his hand into mine. "Yep, although he did have a few glasses of wine earlier. Maybe I should've gotten that in writing."

I just shake my head.

"So, what shirt are you wearing tonight?" I ask as we make our way to the door. "Pink Floyd or—"

He cuts me off. "What makes you think I'm not wearing a dress shirt?"

I glare at him, and he grins. "Okay. You got me. And you got it right on the first guess. Not bad." He winks.

Stepping into the ballroom is like being transported into a different world. I stop for a minute to take in the place. The crystal candelabras everywhere and the fresh cut flowers on each of the tables around the room make the ballroom look stunning, just like it does every year. But my favorite part has really always been the large skylight on the ceiling, allowing for the most breathtaking view of the moon. I've always wondered what it would be like to be in this ballroom when it is empty, just laying down on the floor at night, in silence, staring at the moon. Jace nudges my shoulder with his, leans against me, and whispers, "Ready to go, Cinderella?"

I giggle. "Yes."

Jace and I walk toward the tables filled with drinks and appetizers. On the way there, we say hi to a few people from school. I stop to talk to Zoey, Mr. Mills's granddaughter, and wish her a happy birthday. She's new to our school, so I don't know her well, but she seems nice.

Minutes later, I catch Jace watching me with this sad look in his eyes. I can see the moment he tenses, and just like that, the gut feeling is back.

Jace walks toward me. "Come with me," he whispers, and he leads me through the double doors that take us to the backyard of the mansion. I'm so nervous, I don't even notice our surroundings. I just know that something bad is coming. Jace reaches for my hand and brushes his finger over the infinity symbol on my ring. He just keeps staring at the ring and playing with it, and my anxiety gets the best of me.

"What did you want to talk about?" I ask in a nervous tone.

He gives me a sad smile. "Later," he says.

He reaches for his phone and plugs his headphones in. I give him a puzzled look, and he smiles. He reaches over and puts the headphones in my ears. Nothing is playing at this point. He leans in and gives me a quick kiss before asking me to dance with him.

I blush and look down, avoiding his gaze. This is so like him, to make these big romantic gestures that I can never say no to.

He gently puts his fingers against my chin, tilting my head up. "Close your eyes," he whispers before he pushes play and one of my favorite slow songs comes on. He closes the distance between us, and my eyes drift shut. After a while, I feel the cold snowflakes falling against my skin, and I grin. But it is his laughter that brings me back to the moment. I open my eyes to find him watching me with a grin across his face—showing off his dimples—and there is this sparkle in his eyes.

I memorize every single detail—every single feeling about this moment. The cold. The few seconds of snow, just at the right time. His smile. That look in his eyes. It's almost as if I'm programming myself to memorize everything about this one happy moment.

As if it was my last.

~

HEIDI

MAY 2018

"Jace," I mumble as I open my eyes.

Feeling disoriented, I realize that I'm lying face down on dirt and grass. *Snow . . . What happened to the snow?* I sit, slowly, and look up. The first thing I see is the moon. My head is spinning like crazy. At the sound of something howling, I frantically stand up and look around for my phone. I curse myself for having a black phone case.

"Ugh. I'm never going to find the thing in the dark."

I hear the sound of someone clearing his throat, and for a split second, I feel myself relax, thinking that it is Jace. I spin around—faster than I should—and see a tall dark-haired guy with bright green eyes, leaning against a tree right before me.

"Need help finding something?" he asks with a raspy voice, crossing his arms over his chest.

I take a step back. "Who are you?"

He shrugs and just keeps gawking at me. I haven't seen him at school before. He is the kind of person I would remember seeing. Something about him feels . . . different.

"I'm leaving," I say, and I feel stupid for even having to announce that. I should be running, but my still-spinning head is a huge sign I wouldn't make it far. I turn around and start to walk away slowly, and hope to God he doesn't follow me. *Ugh. I'm always making fun of people in scary movies who try to run and end up getting killed. Please don't let me become a cliché.*

I don't get far before I hear him again.

"Wrong way," he says.

I glance back, and he is at the exact same spot. He points in a completely different direction. I find myself questioning whether to believe him or not, but another howl coming from the direction I'd been heading makes me follow his guidance. I give him a short nod and start walking away. As soon as I'm far enough from his view, I pick

115

up the pace, and with every step, I feel like something is behind me—until I'm out of the woods.

Somehow, I find my way out to where I can see the Mills estate. I keep walking, and I don't stop until I'm in front of the mansion. I stare at it—probably for longer than I should, considering that something is definitely not right. I look down at the long light-blue dress I wore to the ball, then back at the mansion. You can't even tell something happened here tonight. *His smile . . . the snow . . .* I look around, confused. Strange things happen in this town from time to time, but nothing like this. How many hours could have passed?

"My parents are going to freaking ground me for life," I mumble before I turn around and head home.

As I make my way down Eighth Street, it hits me that the Christmas decorations are gone. I shake my head and keep walking. I replay the night in my head over and over. The last thing I remember was Jace and me dancing. He'd have never let me go into those woods alone. When I get to town square, chills creep over my skin. I feel like someone is watching me again, and I start to walk faster. I'm pretty much running by the time I arrive at my front door.

I stop in front of my house and sigh. I reach for the doorknob and slowly turn it, thankful that my parents never lock the door. If I'm lucky enough, they're sleeping.

I slowly close the door behind me. The house is pitch black. *Yes!* I think to myself.

I go straight upstairs to my room. I open the door and wonder where this god-awful lavender smell is coming from. I look at the clock, and it is three in the morning. I think about calling Jace to find out what happened, but remember that my phone is gone. I'm definitely not taking the risk of waking up mom and dad just to use their phones. Without even turning the lights on or bothering to change, I just make my way to bed and lie down. My first thought is that the mattress feels weird, but I quickly dismiss it as me possibly being tired—even though I don't feel tired at all. And then, I turn around and see the shape of a body next to me. I scream bloody murder as I jump up and rush to turn the light on. A familiar girl lies on my bed.

"Rose?" I say. "Hey!" I yell at my cousin.

Nothing. She doesn't even move.

I start to tremble as I walk closer to my bed. I poke her arm once, then again—really hard. She just tosses and turns.

I turn around to go get Mom, but freeze in place when I see my reflection in the mirror. Barely recognizing myself, I take a few steps closer and lean in toward the mirror. My dress is covered in dirt and blood. My gaze goes to the gash on my forehead with dried-up blood surrounding it. The skin around it looks discolored. I lean even closer and lightly touch the gash on my forehead. I feel nothing, and that is when I realize that I must be having one screwed-up dream. This has to be a dream . . .

I poke at the gash on my forehead again. Harder this time.

"That is disgusting." It's the same voice I heard back in the woods, and I spin around to see that guy again. "You won't feel anything," he says as he yawns and sits on my bed.

I should be scared of him. I should be yelling or running, or both, but I feel oddly calm. And honestly, I'm just waiting to wake up at any second and make this all go away.

I glance at Rose, and she's in a deep sleep.

"She can't hear us," he says. His tone is dry and cold, but I can see concern in the way he's watching me, and my stomach drops.

"I'm not dreaming, am I?" I ask, and he shakes his head. I look back at the mirror and stare. "What happened to me?" I whisper, feeling the need to cry, but unable to.

Looking in the mirror, I see him walk closer and stand right next to me. His gaze holds mine through our reflections.

"You died," he says.

Purchase *Avenoir* by Daniele Lanzarotta at your favorite book retailer.

Made in United States
Cleveland, OH
11 December 2024

11674724R10080